# The Junior Novelization

Published in the United States by Random House Children's Books, a division of Random House, Inc., New York, and simultaneously in Canada by Random House of Canada Limited, Toronto, in conjunction with Disney Enterprises, Inc.



Library of Congress Control Number: 2004103556

ISBN: 0-7364-2292-7

Printed in the United States of America
10 9 8 7 6 5 4 3

# The Junior Novelization

Adapted by Irene Trimble

# Chapter 1

About a year ago, in the small town of Oakey Oaks, a young teenaged chicken of unusually small proportions sat contentedly under an oak tree. His name was, appropriately, Chicken Little, and he was enjoying the pleasant day when quite suddenly something of rather large proportions hit him squarely on the head!

*Ouch!* he thought as he rubbed the red comb atop his head. "What in the world was that?"

And then he saw it: just a few feet from where he sat, something shaped a bit like a stop sign, bouncing to the ground. Chicken Little gasped. It was the same color as the sky. It had white shapes on it that looked just like clouds. Chicken Little felt quite sure—no, absolutely positive—this was a piece of the sky. Then the terrible, horrible truth (or so he thought) struck him.

THE SKY WAS FALLING!

Chicken Little knew his duty. He had to warn his dad, his friends, and in fact, the entire town of Oakey Oaks! But how could he do it fast enough to protect them from the falling sky?

There was only one answer: he would go to the school bell tower. It was known throughout the town of Oakey Oaks that if someone rang the school bell, there was an emergency—a big emergency.

Chicken Little took off as fast as his tiny legs could carry him toward the school, where he struggled to the top of the bell tower. Reaching for the rope that rang the bell, he finally managed to grasp it. He began swinging back and forth on it with all his might.

DONG! DONG! DONG! "Run for your lives! Everyone, run for cover!" Chicken Little yelled. "SOS! Mayday! Mayday! Code red! Duck and cover! YOU'RE ALL IN DANGER!"

The townsfolk of Oakey Oaks began to scream and panic. They knew that something must be terribly wrong. A rabbit mother yanked her many bunny children from their carriage so she could rush them to safety. Cars overturned and crashed. Townsfolk ran about, thinking that the world was coming to an end. The terrible words "Run for your lives!" echoed in their ears.

The fire truck raced out of the town's fire station as Chicken Little screamed, "EMERGENCY! EMERGENCY!" from the bell tower. It sped down the main street and nearly hit a car, then swerved so that its ladder swung around and hit a different car. That car spun out of control and hit a fire hydrant, launching the hydrant into the air. The hydrant smacked against the water tower, knocking the huge round water tank to the ground. The tank rolled down the street, crashed through the movie theater, and bounced off three cars, causing more panic as townsfolk ran to get out of its way. The town had been thrown into complete chaos.

Through the sounds of screeching tires and crunching metal, a firefighter called up to the tower, "Chicken Little, what is it? What's going on?"

"The sky is falling! The sky is falling!" Chicken Little yelled.

Suddenly, everything seemed to stop.

"The sky is falling?" asked a rabbit.

"Are you crazy?" someone else asked.

"No, no! It's true!" Chicken Little climbed down from the tower. "Come with me!"

The townsfolk followed him as he ran toward the park in the middle of the town square. "It happened under the old oak tree," he explained to the crowd.

The folks of Oakey Oaks anxiously gathered around as the little chicken scurried through the grass near the tall tree. He was clearly looking for something. He looked everywhere. He searched the ground frantically. But there was no piece of the sky.

Chicken Little began to panic. If he couldn't find the piece of sky, how would he prove to his friends and neighbors that they were in terrible danger? Nobody would believe him if he didn't have the proof!

"I'm not making this up. I know it's here!" he said, looking into the faces of his neighbors.

Chicken Little looked down and muttered, "Th-there's a piece of the sky somewhere . . . somewhere on the ground . . . here." Then he looked up and saw a stop sign. "It was shaped like that!" he shouted, pointing to the sign, hoping against hope that that would provide some kind of proof to the crowd surrounding him.

Every head in the crowd turned. "It looks like a stop sign?" a puzzled dog asked.

"Yes!" Chicken Little said excitedly. Perhaps they would

believe him after all! "Only it doesn't say *stop*. And it's blue and it has a cloud on it. And it hit me on the head." Chicken Little was nodding enthusiastically when an acorn suddenly dropped from the tree and clunked the top of his head.

". . . and it looks like a stop sign," the little chicken said, dizzy and swaying.

Buck Cluck broke through the crowd and picked up the acorn. "Son, is this what hit you?"

"Wha—?" Chicken Little mumbled, still dazed from the knock on his head. He looked up at the huge rooster. "Oh, no, Dad. It was definitely a piece of the sky."

Buck could see that the crowd was becoming impatient. He had to do something.

"Piece of the sky," he mumbled, trying to think of a way out of this. "It's okay, everyone!" he added more loudly, trying to smile. "There's been, like, a little mistake; it was just an acorn that hit my son. A little acorn."

But Chicken Little shook his head. "No, Dad—no!"

"Quiet, son," Buck told Chicken Little in a low voice. "This is embarrassing enough already."

Suddenly, a gaggle of reporters broke through the crowd and surrounded the flustered chicken.

"Chicken Little, what were you thinking?"

"Why would you put your town's safety in jeopardy?"

"How could you mistake a stop sign for an acorn?"

The crowd was silent. Everyone waited to hear Chicken Little's explanation.

# Chapter 2

Poor Chicken Little was so terrified that he could barely speak. When he finally opened his beak, all he could manage to say was "But . . . it was a bigaccorkka . . ." The chicken was clearly crazy. He was making no sense. He could hardly even speak! What was wrong with him?

The crowd began to buzz. "What did he say?" asked one of the reporters.

"But . . . it was a bigaccorkka . . . ," Chicken Little repeated, clearing his throat.

"It was a big acorn?" asked a cub reporter.

"It was an ape throwing coleslaw?" a dog ventured.

"B-but . . . it was a bigaccorkka . . . !" Chicken Little was beginning to get flustered.

Someone in the crowd shouted, "Gesundheit!" No one could even begin to guess what Chicken Little was trying to say. An overwhelmed Chicken Little simply couldn't manage to get the right words out.

"Ladies and gentlemen," a dog reporting the story announced finally, "it's just gibberish."

Chicken Little cringed. But things were about to get worse. The smoke was still rising from the town of Oakey Oaks, and the residents were now steaming mad. Every eye was focused on Chicken Little and his dad.

The town had nearly been destroyed. And it was all because a little chicken had been hit on the head by an acorn? There was no excuse good enough to get Chicken Little off the hook for this mistake.

"Aw, come on, Buck!" Mayor Turkey Lurkey gobbled. "Your kid went and scared us all half to death."

Buck threw his arms into the air. "Well, what can I tell you, folks?"

He followed the crowd as they walked away in disgust. "My son, you know . . . Kids do crazy stuff. You have kids."

Chicken Little was still trying to explain as his father turned to leave. "No, Dad. It wasn't an acorn. It was a piece of the sky. Really, it was!"

But Buck Cluck was not interested in listening to his son.

He simply wanted to go away and hide in embarrassment. How could his own son have done this to him? Chicken Little had nearly destroyed the town, thrown everyone into a panic, talked like a wild chicken, and humiliated himself, not to mention Buck.

Meanwhile, Chicken Little was crushed. Not even his father believed him. Something much bigger than an acorn had hit him on the head. And it had looked like the sky, and it had been shaped kind of like a stop sign. Why wouldn't anyone believe him?

Sadly, he hung his head and began walking. He thought he might take the long route home. Maybe Buck would be asleep by the time Chicken Little went through the front door of the house. That way he wouldn't have to face his humiliated dad.

One year later, Buck was driving Chicken Little to the bus stop as he did every day. The small town of Oakey Oaks proudly displayed a welcome sign that read THE BEST ACORNS IN THE WHOLE UNIVERSE. But today there was something bigger than the little sign. It was a brand-new billboard. Chicken Little's lower beak dropped as he read it: Coming Soon! *Crazy Little Chicken: The Movie*. The signs were all over town. Clearly, Chicken Little had not been able to live down his big mistake.

"Ha! Huh. A movie! A movie. They're making a movie," Buck moaned, blankly staring at the billboards. He shook his head in amazement. "When, when is it gonna end? First the newspaper, then the book, then the book and tape. Then the board game and the little spoons with your face on them. And then the Web site, the commemorative plates . . ."

"Yeah, I saw them," Chicken Little replied quietly. In fact, he remembered them all too well. The plates had images of Oakey Oaks, with horrified townsfolk running for their lives in the background, screaming and yelling.

"You can't eat off them," Buck added, "but they're there."

"Well, they're not microwave safe," Chicken Little said with a frown, "but . . ." His voice trailed off and the two rode in silence.

Buck and Chicken Little held their breath as they saw the old bell tower in the distance. It was where Chicken Little had yelled the words that had changed their lives forever, and now the whole story was going to be a movie.

They passed a dog family happily motoring down the road. All the puppies hung their heads out the back of the truck, their tongues lapping the air. A fish drove by, *glub-glubb*ing in his fishbowl on wheels. All in all, things had pretty much gotten back to normal for the folks of Oakey Oaks: buildings had been rebuilt, streetlamps had been fixed, windows had been replaced. Unfortunately, things had not really gotten back to normal for Chicken Little and his dad.

A chameleon crossing guard turned from green to red. Buck stopped the car. Outside Chicken Little's window, a bird tried to enter a china shop. The bird missed the door and walked smack into the window, falling backward onto the sidewalk. A bit dazed, the bird got up and tried again—*smack!*—walking right into the window. This time the bird didn't get up after it hit the ground.

The bull store owner came out and wiped the smudge off the window. He was clearly unfazed by this type of behavior. Birds and windows—they always seemed to clash.

Buck glanced over at another car. "Ha, there's a bumper sticker. Heh-heh. I knew it was only a matter of time." He sighed. "Billboards I could live with," he muttered. "Posters I could live with. But bumper stickers—it's, like, glued on forever."

As Buck spoke, Chicken Little tried to gather his courage to say something serious to his father. He wanted to turn things around, to make his dad proud of him.

"Heh! Look, it doesn't matter, Dad," he blurted out, "because I have a plan!"

The chameleon turned green, and Buck pulled forward in the car.

Buck looked at his son. "Yeah, about that . . . Remember how I told you it would be better for you just to lie low? Don't call attention to yourself, right?" Buck paused, wondering how to explain. "It's like a game. A game of hide-and-seek. Except the goal is never to be found, ever."

"But—" Chicken Little said. He really believed all he needed was a chance, and then things would turn around for him and his dad.

But Buck cut him off. "Great. Now we've got a plan, right?" Buck said, pulling the car up to the bus stop. "I'll see you later. Remember, lie low."

Chicken Little jumped out of the car and waved as his dad drove away. Then he sighed. He wanted to make his dad proud, but it was hard to see how lying low and hiding would help anything. In fact, if he hid the rest of his life, he would never have a chance to make his dad proud. He would just be a hidden chicken—never seen and never appreciated.

As Chicken Little walked toward his bus stop, a mother dog and her puppy trotted down the sidewalk.

"Look, Mama!" the puppy called out. "There's the crazy chicken!"

"Yes, it is." The mother dog nodded, steering her puppy

away. "You're so smart," she told her pup quickly, hurrying him along. "We don't make eye contact. Buh-bye!" The puppy gaped as his mother yanked him away.

Chicken Little couldn't take it anymore. Things simply had to change. "That's it!" he said firmly as he made his way to the curb, where the school bus was pulling up. "Today is a new day!"

Chicken Little raised one foot to climb onto the bus when a swarm of kids suddenly trampled him to the ground, all racing to get onto the bus first.

He felt one foot after another on his back; then—*hisss*—the bus door slammed shut. Chicken Little got to his feet and ran for it. Maybe, if he was lucky, someone on the bus would see him and ask the bus driver to stop.

Someone did see Chicken Little.

Unfortunately, it was Foxy Loxy, the school bully.

A devilish smile spread across Foxy's face as she looked down from the bus window. Then she held out her hand. Foxy's goofy sidekick, a not-so-bright, not-so-nice gosling named Goosey Loosey, passed Foxy a paper bag.

Foxy tipped the bag out the window, spilling a slew of acorns onto the pavement behind the bus. Chicken Little slipped and slid on the acorns, finally flipping onto his back. He lifted his head. He could see all the kids on the bus laughing as the bus drove off.

It might have seemed hopeless to any other chicken, but Chicken Little was no stranger to obstacles. He'd struggled with them his whole life. First being the smallest kid in his whole class, then having to wear the thickest glasses in his whole school, and now being the subject of a movie that said he was the craziest chicken in the whole world! He wasn't about to take any of it lying down. He sprang to his feet and took off as fast as his little legs would let him. He had to get to school!

Chicken Little made it to the corner, looked up at the traffic signal, and saw the DON'T WALK sign. Cars darted from both directions. How would he get across?

He tried jumping up to reach the pedestrian crossing button, but it was too high. Thinking quickly, the tiny chicken picked a flower and wrapped the stem around the pole. Using this for extra help, he shinned up to the button like a lumberjack. He hit the button with his beak, then dropped to the ground as traffic came to a halt. Then he dashed across the street.

That was when he stepped into another sticky problem—a large wad of gum on the crosswalk. Chicken Little tried mightily to pull his foot free from the gum, but it was no use. The gum stretched and then snapped back, pulling him down. He fell into the sticky wad seat-first.

*Oh, no,* thought Chicken Little as the signal changed again. Traffic was hurtling toward him. Quickly, he grabbed a lollipop from his pocket and licked it as fast as he could. A glistening chrome bumper was barreling toward him!

As the car zoomed over the tiny chicken, he slapped the lollipop onto its rear bumper. The car instantly yanked him free of the sticky gum and launched him to the other side of the road. Chicken Little thrust his arms into the air triumphantly!

Then he looked down. His pants were gone! They were still stuck to the gum in the crosswalk. Poor Chicken Little was standing by the road in only his glasses, a shirt . . . and a pair of bright white underpants. There weren't many worse things in life for a young teenager to face, but Chicken Little, true to character, tried hard to think of a solution—a superfast solution.

Any hope of retrieving his pants (and his dignity) vanished

moments later as a passing truck rolled over them. The sticky bubble gum clung to a tire of the truck, carrying Chicken Little's pants with it. The pants went around and around on the tire until they disappeared down the street.

Horrified by his near nakedness, Chicken Little darted from bush to bush until Oakey Oaks Middle School was finally in sight. He crept up to the building, hoping to enter unnoticed. He spied an open window in the gym, but it was on the second floor. Looking around, he spotted the soda machine and smiled. If anyone knew how to make good use of a bottle of soda pop, it was Chicken Little!

He dropped some money into the machine, took a soda bottle, shook it hard, and strapped it to his back. He removed the cap, and—*whoosh*—the carbonated drink propelled him like a rocket, up and through the window.

Once inside, Chicken Little proudly somersaulted to his feet. He had done it! He had arrived at school without his pants and no one had even noticed.

Then he heard the screams. He had landed—underpants in full view—right in front of a pyramid of cheerleaders in the gym for an early practice. Horrified shrieks from the startled girls filled the giant room as a very embarrassed Chicken Little made a mad dash to escape through the nearest exit.

Panting with exhaustion, Chicken Little raced to his locker. Since the tiny chicken's locker was on the upper level, he had to throw a shoelace up and around the lock in order to jimmy it open. When the door swung open, a small window shade unrolled to the ground. Chicken Little grabbed it and yanked, letting the shade pull him up and into the locker. To him, this was simply a daily routine. But now came the hard part: he had to make himself a pair of pants somehow.

Quickly, he grabbed his math notebook and tore out a page. In moments, he sported a perfectly folded pair of origami paper pants. They might have looked strange, but they fit.

*Yahoo! I made it!* the little chicken thought. But just as he was ready to exit the locker, the school janitor accidentally slammed the door shut with his broom.

A tiny noise was all that could be heard from the locker. It sounded a bit like some shuffling of papers and books, then the clanging of metal against metal. A few moments later, a wire hanger stuck out of the slats in the locker door. Chicken Little was inside, using the hanger as a tool to open the locker door handle. Even the talented chicken had a hard time pulling this one off. It was going to take a while to get the hanger in exactly the right place to open the door.

The 9:00 bell rang. It was official: Chicken Little was late.

# Chapter 5

Mr. Woolensworth was a stodgy old sheep. He taught the first class of the day, Mutton Class, or as it was sometimes called by the students, Everything You Never Wanted to Know About Speaking in Sheep.

"Very well," old Woolensworth said as his students took their seats. He moved his spectacles higher on his nose and began to take attendance.

"Foxy Loxy?"

"Present, pretty, and punctual," thc obnoxious fox answered, happily noting to herself that Chicken Little was late again. Apparently, her acorn trick had worked. It always gave Foxy great pleasure to know that she had succeeded in getting one of her classmates into trouble.

Woolensworth nodded and continued.

"Goosey Loosey?"

A honk came from behind Foxy.

"Master Runt of the Litter?"

Runt, an enormous piglet in a tiny blue jacket, stood up, along with his desk, which his stomach was firmly wedged into.

"Present and accounted for, Mr. Woolensworth," Runt squeaked nervously.

"Loser," coughed Foxy just loudly enough for all of the other students to hear.

Woolensworth picked up his pace. "Henny Penny, Ducky Lucky," he went on. "Morkubine Porcupine!"

"Yo," Morkubine answered.

Woolensworth looked over his spectacles at the bristly young porcupine. Then his eyes returned to the attendance sheet. "Fish Out of Water?" he called.

A fish in a water-filled diver's helmet waved his little fins and blubbed a happy response. Then he mimed pushing a button and did a mini downward dance, pretending to descend in an elevator. Fish enjoyed doing silly things. It made him happy, as most things in life did.

"Abby Mallard?" Woolensworth continued.

"Ugly Duckling," Foxy said under another fake cough. The class broke into a fit of laughter.

"Class, I will not tolerate rude behavior at the expense of a fellow—"

"No worries, Mr. Woolensworth," Abby said, smiling bravely. But as Mr. Woolensworth turned toward Abby, he took one quick look at her and screamed.

"You mustn't sneak up on me," Mr. Woolensworth told her, trying not to hurt her feelings. He cleared his throat. "Where was I?"

"Ugly Duckling," Foxy coughed again, but Abby was unimpressed by the bully's attempts to annoy her.

"Chicken Little," Woolensworth continued, ignoring Foxy's remark. Mr. Woolensworth glanced at Chicken Little's desk.

Foxy promptly coughed loudly, "Tardy again," and smiled. Abby and Runt looked at Chicken Little's empty chair with concern. Where was their friend?

Mr. Woolensworth frowned disapprovingly, then made a mark on his clipboard.

Finally, Mr. Woolensworth closed his attendance book and opened the textbook. "Class," he said, "turn to page sixty-two and translate each word in Mutton.

"She," Mr. Woolensworth prompted.

"BAAAAH," the class translated.

"They," Mr. Woolensworth continued, pacing up and down the aisles. "We."

"BAAH!" the students all said in sheep language as their eyes began to glaze over.

Sometime during second-period gym class, Chicken Little finally escaped from his locker with the help of the wire hanger. He went directly to the gymnasium, where his three best friends, Abby, Runt, and Fish, were already playing a game of dodgeball with the rest of the class.

Fish was having a great time dancing in circles around the gym floor, happily glubbing in the water-filled diver's helmet that covered his head. He dodged the balls without any effort at all.

Runt, on the other hand, made quite a target. It was hard to believe that this nine-hundred-pound pig was the runt of his family's litter. Shrieking in fear, he raced around the dodgeball floor, trying to hide behind his much smaller classmates to avoid being pelted by the balls.

Runt watched in panic as a ball bounced off a bunny's head and whizzed past him. The enormous piglet frantically ran back and forth across the court.

"Calm down, Runt!" Abby yelled. "Just do what Fish is doing."

Runt looked over to see Fish twirling on his tail, dancing and hopping. The balls were missing him every time. Runt gave it a try. He raised his large body up and began to spin. Suddenly, he squealed. Every ball in the gym seemed to be bouncing off him.

Chicken Little slipped in beside Abby, keeping a sharp eye on the balls flying from every direction. Abby took a look at his origami pants. "Tough morning?" she asked.

He nodded. "I had a run-in with my old nemesis."

Abby raised an eyebrow and smiled. "Gum in the crosswalk?"

Chicken Little nodded. "He won this round."

"Incoming on your right," Abby said calmly to Chicken Little. The two hopped over a ball together. Abby kept her eye on the court. "I heard about the movie," she told him. "Tough break. Hey, maybe it'll just go straight to video."

"That's the least of my problems," Chicken Little said breathlessly. "This morning my dad told me I should basically just disappear." He tried to remain positive. "But you know, that's not going to get me down, because I've got a plan. You want to hear about it?"

Abby looked at him. "Uh-oh."

"No, no, no, no," Chicken Little said quickly, knowing what she was thinking. "This one's good. Look, one moment destroyed my life, right? One moment."

He paused to jump aside as a ball sped directly at them. "Warthog at three o'clock!" he warned Abby.

"So I figure all I need is a chance—" Chicken Little was interrupted again as another ball shot by him. "All I need is a chance to do something great to make everyone forget the whole sky-falling thing once and for all. And then my dad will finally have a reason to be proud of me."

Just then, the coach blew his whistle.

"Time-out!" he called. There were half a dozen balls stuck to Morkubine's quills. "Nurse!" the coach shouted as he led the porcupine toward the door.

Given a moment to relax, all the other kids in the gym class immediately whipped out their cell phones.

"So what do you think?" Chicken Little asked Abby. He was still thinking about his plan.

The duck looked at Chicken Little. It was time to tell him what she really thought. "Okay, listen. You said the sky was falling. Your dad didn't support you. And you have been hurting inside ever since. Right?"

"Well . . . ," Chicken Little said. He was a bit taken aback by Abby's bluntness. "B-but—"

"No b-buts!" Abby said forcefully. "Here's the main thing: you have got to stop messing around and deal with the problem. Here's the real solution: you and your dad . . . talk, talk, talking . . . closure."

"Closure?" said Chicken Little.

"Talking about something until it's resolved," explained Abby. She turned and started pulling magazines out of her backpack. "Wait, hold on," she said, holding up a magazine with a very trendy teen duck on the cover. Abby seemed sure the magazine articles could help.

"I told you, I have a plan," pleaded Chicken Little.

Still, Abby insisted on rattling off quotes from her teen magazine advice columns: "You should 'stop the squawk and try the talk,'" she said. "'Avoiding closure with your parents can cause early molting.' See?" Abby pointed to a headline in the magazine. "Closure."

Chicken Little heaved a sigh. He knew she was just trying to help, but the problem was that nobody—not Abby, not even his dad—seemed to understand him.

"Abby, listen," he said, "talking is a waste of time. I've got to do something great so my dad doesn't think I'm such a loser."

As far as Chicken Little was concerned, his dad's respect meant more than anything else.

"C'mon!" Abby said. "You are not a loser! You're inventive and resourceful and funny and cute and . . ." As Abby began to drift along with her emotions, Chicken Little started to get uncomfortable with what she was saying. Was it possible? Did she maybe . . . have a crush on him?

Suddenly, Abby snapped out of it. Both friends froze in place. Abby rapidly changed the subject. "Uh, Runt, should Chicken Little have a good talk with his dad and clear the air?" She smiled widely to make sure Runt knew this was the correct answer. "Or keep searching for bandage solutions in a denial-based dance of masculine dysfunction?" She frowned dramatically to let Runt know this was definitely *not* the right answer.

"Bandage solutions," Runt replied.

"Runt!" Abby rolled her eyes in frustration.

"I'm sorry!" Runt defended himself. "I'm very bad at reading facial cues!"

Abby had already turned her attention to Fish.

"Fish! Help me out here," she pleaded.

But Fish was too busy clinging to the top of a paper tower he had happily been building out of Abby's magazine pages. Now he was at the top of the tower, waving away imaginary airplanes that he pretended were attacking him. The paper tower quickly crashed to the floor, taking Fish with it. Unhurt, he smiled and glubbed.

"Men!" Abby commented with disgust.

Suddenly, Foxy Loxy hurled a ball at Abby. The squishy dodgeball slapped Abby in the face with such force that it knocked her off her feet. As Abby's three friends ran to help her, Foxy sneered.

"Hahahahahaha!" came the cries of laughter from the rest of the class. But not from Runt or Fish. And definitely not from Chicken Little.

"That does it!" the chicken shouted. Standing tall (or at least as tall as a tiny chicken can), Chicken Little marched right over to Foxy. "We were in a time-out, Foxy. Prepare to hurt!"

Foxy snapped her fingers. Goosey bolted into action. She grabbed Chicken Little by the comb on his head and quickly shook him a few times. Then she stretched the comb back like a rubber band and launched him slingshot-style across the gym. Chicken Little hit the window with a splat.

Runt, Fish, and Abby rushed to help him, but Goosey blocked the way.

As Chicken Little slid down the glass, he grabbed a T-shaped handle at the bottom of the window to stop his fall. He hung for a second as Runt, Fish, and Abby held their breath. The handle peeled downward, with Chicken Little still clinging to it.

A blaring siren filled the gym as the sprinkler system went off. Chicken Little cringed. He'd just pulled the fire alarm!

Humiliated and helpless, he dangled from the handle as water from the overhead sprinklers filled his little origami pants and washed them away. For the second time that day, Chicken Little found himself without pants.

In Principal Fetchit's office, Buck Cluck faced the large dog who was reading the list of his son's offenses.

"Not showing for class, inappropriate school attire, picking fights in gym class—and the fire alarm!" Fetchit barked angrily. "Ever since that sky-falling incident, he's been nothing but trouble!"

Chicken Little sat on the bench outside Principal Fetchit's office. Through the principal's frosted-glass window, he could see the silhouette of his father pleading with Mr. Fetchit. The tiny chicken sank lower in his seat. He had embarrassed his father again.

"Now, look, Buck," Fetchit continued, "you know I have the utmost respect for you. You were Buck 'Ace' Cluck, our school baseball star."

Chicken Little looked up and stared at the school trophy case. It was filled with sports trophies and awards with his father's name on them: Buck "Ace" Cluck.

"But let's face the facts," Fetchit continued. "Your kid, he's nothing like you at all."

Buck nodded wearily. "Okay, thank you for talking to me. I'll take care of my son," he mumbled as he turned and walked out the door.

"Dad, it wasn't my fault," Chicken Little said, hopping off the bench. The tiny chicken struggled to keep up with his dad as they walked out of the building. "It was Foxy. She's always trying—"

"That's all right." Buck sounded completely defeated. "It's fine. You don't have to explain anything."

Outside, father and son climbed into the car. The tension became unbearable as they headed home in silence. Finally, Chicken Little cleared his throat, gathering up his courage to speak to Buck.

"Uh, hey, Dad? I was thinking, yeah. What if I, um, what if I joined the baseball team?"

*Screeech!* Buck was so shocked he almost lost control of the car. He hit the brakes and swerved, almost hitting another car. Chicken Little nearly tipped over in the backseat.

"Watch where you're going!" the other motorist yelled.

"Sorry there, buddy!" Buck shouted out his window. "Sorry, sorry."

He turned back to Chicken Little. "Baseball? Son, we talked about this."

"Yeah, right," the little chicken agreed. "But, y'know, that was when I was small. I put on five ounces this year." Chicken Little raised his tiny arm and made a little muscle. "I've really bulked up."

"Really, son? Baseball? Are you sure?"

"Oh, yeah," Chicken Little said enthusiastically. "I mean, you know, hey, why not?"

"But, son, you know, um . . . I'm just wondering, maybe baseball isn't exactly your thing, you know? Have you considered the chess team? Or the glee club? And then some teenagers, you know, they get quite a rush from stamp collecting. You wanna stop? We'll get some stamps."

"No," Chicken Little said firmly. "I don't like stamps."

"All colors, colorful things," Buck said enthusiastically, hoping Chicken Little would choose anything but baseball.

"No, I was thinking—I was thinking baseball! I can't wait

to see the look on your face when I smack that ball in for a touchdown! Ha-ha!"

Buck sighed heavily.

"Dad, *um,* I'm kidding. That was a joke."

Buck shook his head. "Just do me one favor, son?"

"Sure, Dad. Anything."

"Just please try not to get your hopes too high."

Chicken Little nodded sadly. But deep down, he was still ready to fix what had gone wrong the year before. And he felt sure that his playing baseball would make his father proud. This was his new plan. It was his ticket to reversing his one big mistake, to making everyone forget about the sky-falling incident once and for all. All he needed was a big hit, or maybe a big catch, and soon he would be the town hero. At the very least, he could do something to make his dad proud.

That night at the Cluck home, Buck Cluck wearily entered the living room alone. He sadly gazed at a framed picture of himself as a young rooster along with a newly hatched Chicken Little and his departed wife, Chloe.

“Oh, Chloe!” Buck sighed and shook his head sadly. “If only you were here. You’d know what to do.”

At the same time, upstairs, Chicken Little was climbing out his bedroom window onto the roof. He gazed up at the stars. He believed with all his heart that things could be different for him and his dad.

“C’mon,” Chicken Little said to one particularly bright star. “All I need is a chance.”

It wasn't long before baseball season arrived in Oakey Oaks.

When the team sign-up sheet was posted at school, Chicken Little rushed to add his name to the list. Soon he was a member of the Acorns' baseball team, and he couldn't have been prouder.

But during the first game, when it was Chicken Little's turn to bat, the coach stopped him before he even got to the plate. Instead, the bat was handed to Foxy Loxy. With a smirk, Foxy strolled to the plate, pointed to left field, and slammed the ball over the fence for a home run. She loped around the bases and came home to cheers and high fives from her entire team. But when Chicken Little leaped up for his high five, she yanked her hand away, letting him fall face-first into the dirt.

It was the beginning of a pattern that would last almost the entire season for Chicken Little. He hardly ever got a chance to play ball (except for occasionally being placed deep in the outfield). He was always being ignored by his fellow team members, especially Foxy. And he was getting awfully uncomfortable sitting on the bench for the entire nine innings of nearly every game. It was almost . . . boring.

Looking on, Abby cringed at seeing her friend struggle. It was time for some serious training, and Abby knew just where to find the help Chicken Little needed. She scanned the newsstand until she found a magazine on baseball. She smiled as she looked at the powerful sports heroes on the glossy pages. Abby felt sure that with a little guidance from the magazine, and some coaching from his friends, Chicken Little could be a great baseball player, too.

The training program began. Abby had Chicken Little run all the way to school next to Runt's bike every day. He bench-pressed doughnuts on a pencil until his muscles quivered. Chicken Little had to work hard to build up his tiny body, but it was worth it. His reward would be a spot in the Acorns' starting lineup.

In the Acorns' next game, Chicken Little took a place far into the outfield.

Suddenly, a ball flew toward him. *I got it, I got it,* Chicken Little thought happily. But a flash of sunlight blinded him for a second, and—*bonk!*—the ball hit him on the head. Once again, he had lost a big chance to do something right. Instead, Foxy dove into the grass behind Chicken Little and caught the ball as it ricocheted off his head. She even managed a flashy smile as the photographer for the local paper snapped her photo.

That night at the Cluck home, Buck sat at the table reading the sports section—and there was the photo of Foxy making her big catch off Chicken Little's head. Buck sighed as he saw his little son's dizzy expression in the picture.

Chicken Little was disappointed to see the photo, but he felt more determined, too. He would train even harder, he decided. He would show the townsfolk of Oakey Oaks what he was made of!

# Chapter 10

In spite of his extra training, Chicken Little still couldn't convince the baseball coach to give him a chance. Game after game, Chicken Little sat on the bench.

Meanwhile, Foxy wowed the crowds with homer after homer. The papers were calling her a hero and the key to the Acorns' race to make it to the play-offs.

Sure enough, it wasn't long before beautiful old Oakey Oaks Stadium was decked out for the big championship game against longtime rivals the Spud Valley Taters. The stands were filled to capacity. It was going to be a huge day for every player on the Acorns' team except for Chicken Little. His official position was benchwarmer, with no chance to bat. Ever.

He sat in his well-worn spot on the bench, holding his tiny pink glove, as the Acorns' team mascot led the screaming crowd in a cheer. Even Mayor Turkey Lurkey gobbled along. "Lean to the left, lean to the right! C'mon, Acorns, fight, fight, fight!"

His face and body painted in red and white, the Acorns' colors,

Fish robot-danced excitedly along with the mascot. Runt and Abby were perched on the scoreboard, keeping count of every run.

"There's excitement in the air, ladies and gentlemen," the dog announcer said into his microphone. "Yes, it's been two decades since Oakey Oaks has beaten longtime rivals the Spud Valley Taters."

Buck Cluck sat high in the stands and couldn't help remembering that it was his home run that had won the game against the Taters twenty years earlier.

On this day, both ball teams battled just as hard as they had during that long-ago game. The crowd cheered through every inning as the Acorns and the Taters kept the score close.

By the ninth inning, the crowd could hear the tension in the announcer's voice. "And now, down by only a single run, and with a player in scoring position, we finally have a chance again!" The dog could hardly contain himself as he continued talking into the mike. "This excitement isn't just about the fun of baseball, it's not about the prize, it's about the gloating and rubbing their noses in it—the *nah-nah-na-na-na we beat you* taunting, if you will, that comes with winning!" The tension was clearly mounting. “That’s right, folks. Oakey Oaks and the Honorable Mayor Turkey Lurkey will finally have bragging rights again for one full year!” The mayor grinned gleefully. Now, that would make him proud: being the mayor of a town whose team was the league champion!

“But this battle has taken a heavy toll on our hometown heroes.” The dog announcer loosened his collar. “After nine grueling innings and several players out with injuries, the Acorns are scraping the bottom of the roster.”

The dog panted nervously. “Hopefully there’s just enough muscle on the bench to pull out a win.”

Every eye in the stands traveled down the Oakey Oaks Acorns’ bench . . . past the three dogs in neck cones, past the empty spot, all the way to the very end of the bench. And there sat Chicken Little. He was the only uninjured player left.

“Up next,” the dog said, “Chicken Little!”

The cheering stopped.

The crowd gasped as Chicken Little put on a batting helmet that was so big on him it flopped around his head, blocking his view. Chicken Little wobbled to the bat rack. Pulling out a wooden bat, he stumbled backward as the rest of the bats toppled on top of him.

"Clearly a long shot, folks," the announcer said, worried. "Little hasn't been up to bat once since joining the team."

A cheetah in the stands stood and yelled, "He's gonna lose the game for us!"

"But," the announcer continued, "if he can just get a walk and advance to first, that powerhouse Foxy Loxy can step up and save us all."

Foxy Loxy proudly waved to the crowd, soaking up the admiration. The fans immediately began to cheer for their team's best player.

"She's had a terrific game so far," the announcer said. "A shoo-in for the MVP trophy."

As Chicken Little left the dugout, the coach leaned over with some batting advice. "You have an itty-bitty, teeny-tiny strike zone," he said. "There's no way he can throw you out. Just take the walk; don't swing."

"But, Coach," Chicken Little answered hopefully, "I have a good feeling—"

"Just take the walk!" the coach yelled. "Don't swing!"

As the tiny player stepped out, the announcer described his every move to the anxious crowd. "Nervous, gangly, barely able to hold the pine, Little advances to the box."

The weight of the bat caused Chicken Little to sway over home plate. "He's going to bat from the right," the announcer called. "Make it the left," he said as Chicken Little swayed to the other side of the plate. "No, the right."

The umpire, a huge horse, finally put his hoof on Chicken Little's head and kept him from moving.

The announcer nodded, certain at last. "The right."

"Easy out," the Taters' pitcher, a long-legged stork, called to his outfielders with a snicker.

Indeed, the entire Tater team took one look at Chicken Little and figured they had won the game. By the time Chicken Little was steady at the plate, barely holding on to his enormous bat, the Taters in the outfield had lost interest. They knew he'd strike out. The dog in left field began chasing his tail. The bull in center field dropped his mitt and began grazing in the outfield. The mole in right field dug a hole and disappeared altogether.

“Play ball!” the umpire shouted.

“Why him?” moaned the cheetah in the stands. “Why now?”

Buck put his face in his hands and shook his head from side to side with worry.

“I won’t embarrass you, Dad,” Chicken Little whispered when he saw Buck’s head drop. “Not this time.”

“Here’s the windup,” the announcer called, “the pitch . . . ”

The ball whizzed by, high above Chicken Little’s head. The announcer called, “It’s a high cutter—”

*“Ballll!”* the umpire yelled.

The ball smacked into the catcher’s glove. Then Chicken Little swung the bat. He had been struggling madly to swing the heavy bat and had finally managed to do so. But he was so late that he swung into the empty air.

The crowd gasped. Buck groaned.

“Uh . . . strike one?” the umpire said.

The crowd began to boo, but Chicken Little dug in for the next pitch.

“The catcher lays down the signals,” the dog said. “Here’s the pitch. Curveball low and outside—he swings!”

“Strike two!” the umpire yelled.

The crowd screamed, “Don’t swing! Don’t swing!”

“That’s two in the hole,” the announcer said. “One more strike, it’s a punch-out, folks, and we’re all going home.”

Chicken Little concentrated as the pitcher wound up for the third time. “Today is a new day,” Chicken Little said to himself as the ball sped toward him.

He squinted hard and swung with all his might. The crack of the bat could be heard all over Oakey Oaks. The crowd was astonished. Buck couldn't believe his eyes. He looked at the ball sailing into the outfield.

"Take away my squeaky toy! It's a hit!" the dog howled, clutching the microphone.

Chicken Little fell into his batting helmet. "A hit?"

"A hit?" the mayor gobbled as the ball bounced off a sleeping dog in the outfield and bonked the grazing Tater bull on the head.

"But wait," the announcer called frantically, "the batter is still unbelievably at home plate. He's standing in a daze. Run, kid, run!"

Chicken Little jumped out of his batting helmet, which bounced back onto his head. He began to run as he heard Buck yell, "Go, son! Run! Run!"

The only problem was that Chicken Little was running

toward third base instead of first base.

"There he goes," the announcer yelled, "headed the wrong way! Wait, wait, wait!"

"N-n-no!" Buck shouted at the top of his lungs. "Not that way! Run the other way!"

"Turn around!" Abby yelled from the scoreboard. Finally, Chicken Little got the message and turned around.

"Wait, wait, wait!" the announcer roared as Chicken Little made it back to home plate and turned toward first base. Right behind him, Goosey Loosey stepped on home. "We have a tie game!" the dog shouted.

"Today's a new day! Today's a new day!" Chicken Little repeated to himself as he rounded first base.

"Meanwhile, they're scrambling in the alley," the dog announcer called out as all the Spud Valley Taters ran for the ball. The mole popped out of his hole. The bull stopped grazing and began to charge. The dog outfielder stopped chasing his tail and began paying attention to the game.

"Looks like Rodriguez has it. No, it's the center fielder!" the dog said as he saw both the mole and the bull reach for the ball at the same time. In all the confusion, the bull grabbed the mole instead of the ball and hurled him toward second base.

"Mayhem in the outfield, ladies and gentlemen, as Rodriguez is fired to second. Catch is complete, but where's the ball?" The dog talked excitedly as the crowd scanned the field, trying to keep up with what was happening.

The announcer could hardly control himself. "Little touches the bag and keeps going. It's a hunt for the rock. The fielders are having a little trouble. Some kind of commotion out there."

The Spud Valley Taters dove headfirst into a pile as they all scrambled for the ball. When the dust cleared, the ball was stuck on the bull's horn.

"Tip the cow! Tip the cow!" the Taters in the outfield yelled as they pushed the bull over and carried him toward the infield.

"Oh, it's the old tip-the-cow play, as the kid heads for the hot corner," the announcer said to the crowd while Chicken Little ran to third base. "Looks like a stand-up triple!"

"Yes!" Buck yelled along with the cheering crowd.

But Chicken Little didn't stop at third base. And the Taters were picking up some speed as they ran with the bull on their shoulders. Both the bull and the baseball stuck to his horn were getting closer to home plate. Chicken Little was taking a real risk. He could end up being the town hero—or keeping his place as the town zero. It seemed as if all the townsfolk were on their feet. What was the tiny crazy chicken doing?

"Hold up," the announcer shouted. "Incredible!" he said as Chicken Little ran for home. "He's still going for the whole enchilada! The entire ball of wax! The kit and caboodle!"

Foxy ran alongside Chicken Little. "Go back, go back!" she yelled at him. "You're never going to make it!"

The huge brown bull mooed as his head moved toward home plate.

Chicken Little threw off his batting helmet and ran faster.

"The kid's got gumption!" the announcer called. "He's trying to lighten his load. With the entire outfield behind him, Little's on all cylinders now! He slides for the dish. Here comes the center fielder! It's going to be a photo finish at home!"

The bull, with the ball still stuck to his horn, and the little chicken collided at home plate as a cloud of dust covered them. The standing crowd stood motionless, waiting breathlessly for the umpire's call. No one could tell whether Chicken Little was actually touching home plate. There was too much dirt heaped on top of him.

"You're out!" the ump yelled as the bull leaned his huge head down and tapped Chicken Little with the ball. The crowd gasped. Chicken Little must have just missed touching the plate.

"Oh, folks! Folks, what a heartbreaker!" the dog moaned as Runt, Abby, and Fish tried to hold back their tears. Buck covered his face.

"Wait!" the dog suddenly shouted as the umpire pulled a whisk broom from behind his chest protector. He began to dust off Chicken Little, who was up to his neck in dirt.

"Wait a cotton-pickin' second," the dog howled. "Hold your horses here, and horses hold your breath. This might not be over!"

The fans watched from the edges of their seats as the umpire dusted the plate. At last he got all the way down to Chicken Little's foot. It was just touching the corner of home plate.

"Safe!" the ump yelled. "The runner is safe!"

The crowd went crazy.

"It's all over, folks," the dog panted, exhausted. "The Acorns have done the impossible! For the first time in twenty years, we won the pennant! Mothers, kiss your babies, you've witnessed a miracle! Remember where you were at this moment—the smells, the sounds . . ."

Abby proudly flipped the final numbers on the scoreboard while Foxy stood on the field and watched the crowd rush past her toward Chicken Little.

"There's a new winner in town, and his name is Chicken Little!" the dog announcer howled in the background. "This is one memory you'll savor forever!"

"Wait! Wait a second!" Foxy shouted. "That was just a lucky hit!"

Foxy watched in shock as her cheering teammates raised a huge container of sports drink and poured it over Chicken Little's head. The poor little guy was washed away in a gush of fluid a moment later. Luckily, the team found the soaking chicken and lifted him onto their shoulders.

Runt, Abby, and Fish rushed the field to find their best friend and new town hero.

Up in the stands, Buck nearly broke into tears of joy as his very happy son was tossed up and down by his teammates.

"Yes, yes, yes!" Buck laughed. "That's my boy out there! That's my boy!"

Later that night, at the Cluck home, Chicken Little grabbed a spoon for a microphone and sang a victory song to himself. He hopped onto his bedroom windowsill and threw his arms out in triumph.

Buck excitedly peeked through the door. He slipped Chicken Little's baseball glove on and started to replay the final moments of the big game.

"Here's the windup . . . and the pitch!" he called to his son.

Chicken Little grabbed a ruler and held it up like a bat. "It's a knuckleball right down the middle!"

"He swings!" Buck cried, grinning.

"CRACK!"

"It's going . . ."

"He rounds first!" Chicken Little shouted as he ran around his room. "Then on to second!"

"It hits high off the wall!" Buck shouted, too.

"He flies past third and heads for the plate!"

"It's a mad scramble for the ball," Buck said, imitating the dog who had announced the game. "There's the throw home! It's gonna be close! He is . . . SAFE!"

Buck let out a victory whoop.

"Hey! The mighty Acorns win! The mighty Acorns win!" the proud father shouted.

Buck made crowd noises as the two danced around Chicken Little's room.

Finally, Buck fell back on Chicken Little's bed and tried to catch his breath. "I guess that puts the whole sky-is-falling incident behind us once and for all, eh, kiddo?"

Chicken Little smiled. "You bet, Dad!"

After a long pause, he thought of Abby's advice and continued awkwardly, "Unless . . . you think we need closure."

"Closure?" Buck asked, suddenly looking a little uncomfortable. "What's to close here? Unless you think we need to . . . ?"

"No, no!" Chicken Little said quickly. He wished he hadn't even brought up the topic. "Not me!"

"It's closed!" Buck laughed in relief.

"I agree!" Chicken Little said.

"Shut tight!" Buck said.

"Vacuum-sealed!" The little chicken nodded.

Buck paused. "Good!" he said.

"Great, Dad! Closure . . . I dunno. *Pffft!*"

Buck rumpled Chicken Little's head feathers and tried to sit up. "All right. Enough fun," Buck said. "I gotta go."

The overweight rooster struggled to lift his huge body off the bed.

"I—I'll give you a push," Chicken Little said, blinking behind his glasses.

Buck nodded and Chicken Little rocked the rooster until his feet touched the ground.

"There!" Buck said, standing. "Okay, I'm up. I'm up."

Buck walked to the door. "Hey, g'night, Ace."

Chicken Little beamed with pride. His dad had called him Ace, Buck Cluck's very own nickname from when he had played ball.

Chicken Little had never been happier in his whole life. *"Woo hoo!"* he said to himself, cheering. He hopped up on his bed and ran around.

*"Yee hah-hah-hah-hah hoo!"* he yelled, bouncing up to his bedroom window.

Then, quietly, Chicken Little turned his gaze up toward the sky. "Thanks," he said sincerely to the twinkling stars. "Thanks for the chance."

But as he continued looking up at the sky, one particular star seemed to grow brighter and brighter. Chicken Little took off his glasses, wiped the lenses, and put them back on to get a better look.

It looked as if a star were coming straight toward him. But it couldn't happen again—

*Wham!* The star flew through the window and knocked Chicken Little down. He was nearly flattened by a strange metal panel with wires on one side and a bright star on the other. He scrambled out from under it and dove behind his bed. The metal panel creaked and clanged to the floor. Chicken Little gasped. It could mean only one thing.

"NOOOOOOOO!!!!!!" Chicken Little howled, his whole body trembling.

Chicken Little couldn't believe it.

"A piece of the sky? Shaped like a stop sign? Not again!"

Downstairs, Buck was standing at the stove making some popcorn when he heard the commotion.

"Hey! Son! You all right?" he called, throwing the popcorn into the air.

Covered with popcorn, Buck rushed upstairs.

"I'm coming! I'm coming! I'm coming upstairs!"

With his heart pounding, Chicken Little took a blanket and threw it over the panel. There was absolutely no way he wanted his dad to see a piece of the sky in his room. He had had enough sky-falling problems the year before.

"Hey, what's wrong?" Buck asked, bursting through the bedroom door.

"Nothing!" Chicken Little answered with a frozen smile.

"You sure?" Buck asked. "I thought I heard you yell."

Chicken Little shrugged. He was struggling to think of a

reasonable explanation for his sudden scream.

"I—I, uh . . . fell out of bed!" he said weakly.

"Huh? How'd you get over there?" Buck asked, scratching his head. His son was nowhere near the bed.

Chicken Little pretended not to understand the question.

"Over where?" he asked feebly, trying to avoid answering.

"There," Buck said, pointing at him.

Chicken Little hesitated. "Where?" he asked again, looking around his bedroom.

"There! How'd you get over there?" Buck was totally confused.

Chicken Little pushed his glasses up on his beak. "Who we talking about?" he asked finally, looking at his dad.

"Heh-heh. Never mind. What's the difference? Look, the past is behind us, right?

"Tomorrow's gonna be a new day," Buck said.

"Mmm-hmm," Chicken Little agreed. He heaved a sigh of relief as Buck closed the door, knowing his father had not seen the strange object lying on his bedroom floor.

When he was sure his father was gone, Chicken Little slowly reached for a corner of the blanket. His little hand was

Chicken Little is a small chicken with very big dreams.

Abby is Chicken Little's best friend.

Chicken Little wishes for one good thing to happen in his life.

Chicken Little hits a home run!

Buck and his son sing a victory song.

Oh no, the sky is falling – again!

Fish gets carried away!

Abby doesn't have a good feeling about the stadium's flashing lights.

Things start to get really weird!

The friends brave the inside of the spaceship to save Fish.

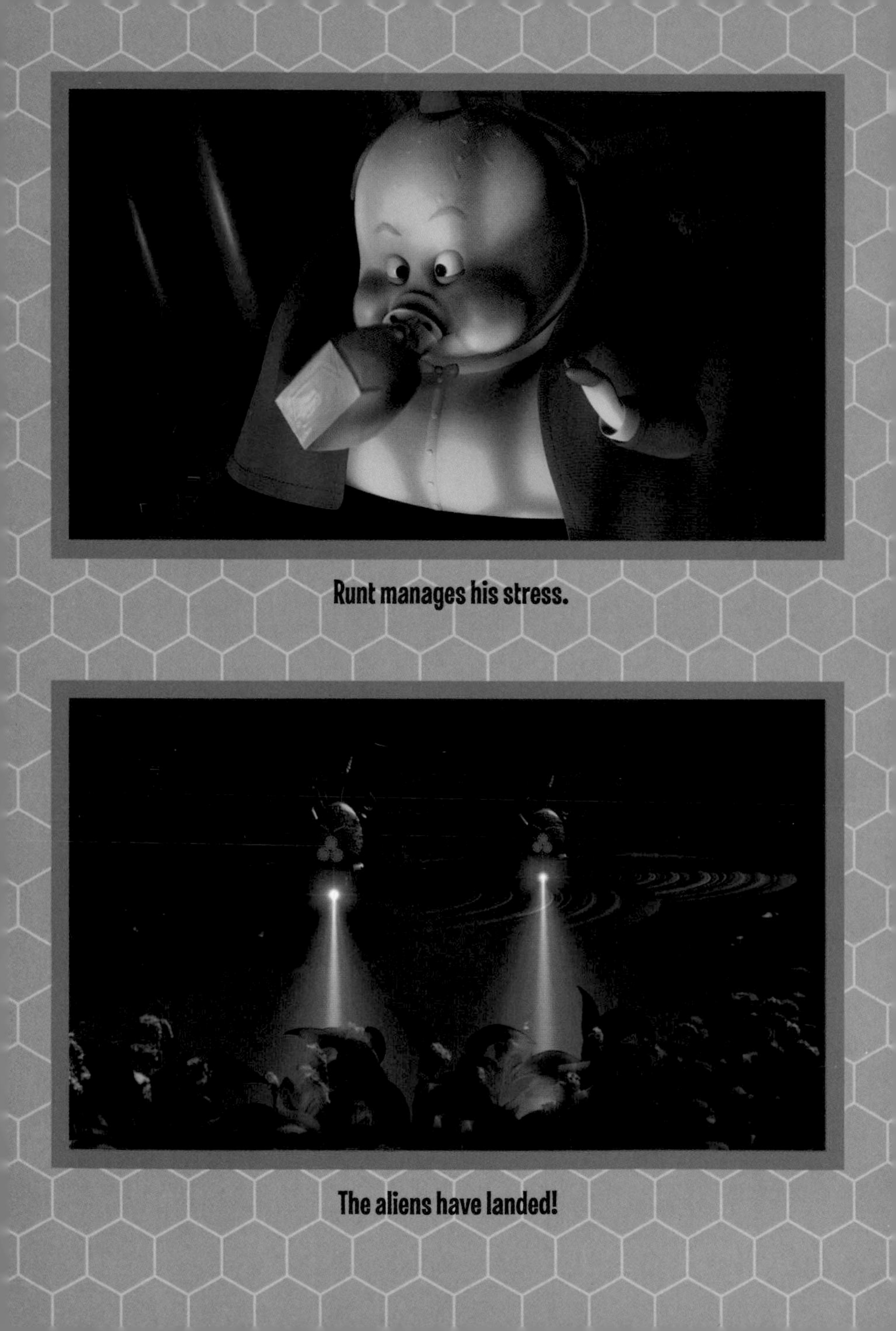

Runt manages his stress.

The aliens have landed!

Spaceships swarm over Oakey Oaks.

Chicken Little rings the bell to warn the town.

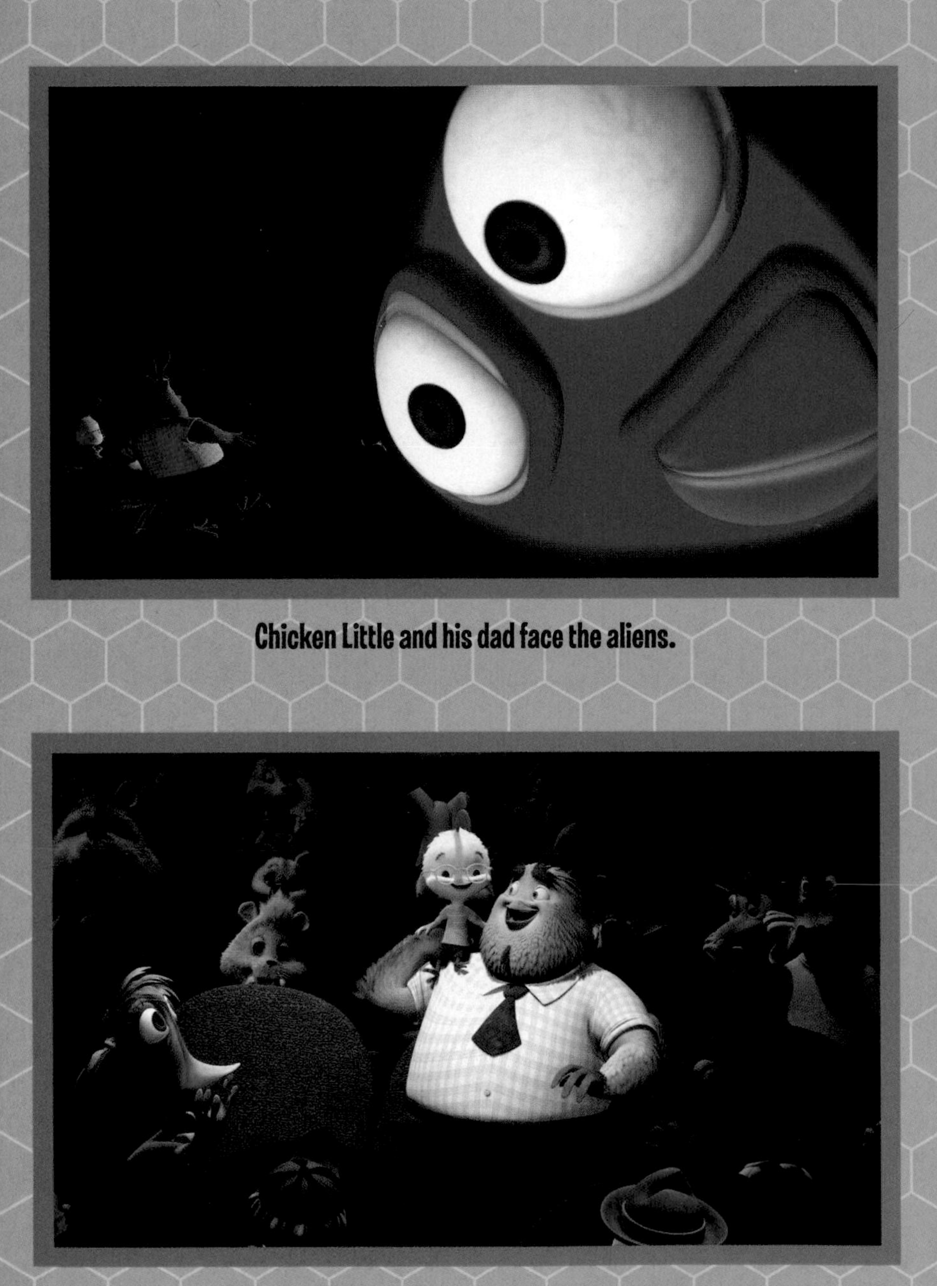

Chicken Little and his dad face the aliens.

Chicken Little becomes the hero of Oakey Oaks!

trembling. He chanted to himself, “Please be gone, please be gone, please be gone!”

He mustered up all his courage. He pressed his eyes shut and, in a swift matador-like sweep, pulled the blanket away.

# Chapter 14

Taking a few deep breaths, Chicken Little popped his eyes open. It was gone! The panel was gone! He wasn't quite sure what had happened, but at least everything was back to normal.

He happily took a step forward when—*clunk*—he suddenly tripped. Chicken Little jumped up and ran to hide behind his backpack. Then he slowly peeked around it.

Finally, the little chicken gathered up all his courage and walked toward the middle of the room. Slowly, he moved his foot along the floor ahead of him. He was feeling around for the missing piece of sky.

When his foot hit something, he reached down and poked it with his finger. He saw an outline of the panel. It flickered for a second and then disappeared. It had cloaked itself—just like a chameleon—blending in with the floorboards, so it actually looked like a part of the floor. Chicken Little jumped back.

Finally, he reached for the panel and picked it up. He turned it over. The back was covered with wires and flashing lights. He carefully lifted the panel and carried it to his window. He held it up . . . and it suddenly blended in with the night sky—stars and all—just as it had with his floor.

Chicken Little dropped the panel and ran out of his room in a panic. "I've got to call Abby!" he cried anxiously.

Meanwhile, at Abby's house, Runt, Fish, and Abby were celebrating the Acorns' big win. They were also celebrating the fact that one of their fellow outcast friends had become the new town hero! Runt and Abby sang karaoke while Fish waved a green light stick over his head and moved to the music. The three were dancing up a storm when Abby's phone rang.

"Hello, Mallard residence," Abby said, trying to raise her voice over the commotion.

Runt continued to celebrate, dancing and singing, completely oblivious to Abby.

"Runt!" Abby said. "Quiet! I'm on the phone!"

But the pig was so into the music and singing that he didn't notice. He just kept dancing and twirling and—

*"Runt!"* yelled Abby finally.

Completely humiliated, Runt at last realized that the song had stopped and he needed to end his performance.

"Hey, where are you?" Abby said into the phone to Chicken Little. "We already started; we were just—" Abby's eyes suddenly bulged. *"What?"* she yelled. She dropped the phone and ran out.

Moments later, Abby, Runt, and Fish rushed into Chicken Little's room. Chicken Little was holding the piece of sky by his side. Abby, Runt, and Fish watched, dumbfounded, as Chicken Little demonstrated how the panel blended perfectly into the wall behind it.

Abby got right to the point.

"Okay," she said. "Let me guess. You haven't told your dad yet."

"Abby, please," begged the desperate chicken. "This is exactly what fell on me the first time. There is no way I'm bringing it up with him again."

Meanwhile, Fish was examining the panel. First he held it up to his face, waiting until the panel showed his image. Then he moved it in front of Abby's face—making it look as if his head were on Abby's body.

Abby pushed the panel out of her face.

"Okay," she said, relenting. "I'm sure there's a simple, logical explanation. I mean, it could be a piece of a weather balloon."

"I just want it out of my life," Chicken Little replied, "gone for good, everything back to normal."

Abby nodded sympathetically at him and thought for a moment.

"Hey, remember when that icy blue stuff fell from the sky and, like, everybody thought it was from space and stuff?" she asked. "And it just turned out to be frozen pee from a jet airplane."

"Yeah, that's right," Runt said excitedly. "It's frozen pee. Yeah, it's frozen pee." He danced around the room, shouting, "Pee pee pee pee!"

Chicken Little couldn't stand it any longer.

"I don't care what it is!" he yelled. "Are you gonna help me get rid of it or not?"

Fish was still playing with the panel when he suddenly noticed a button in the center. He pushed it.

Instantly, the panel began to shimmer and shake. Glowing, it rose and hovered in the air. Happily unfazed, Fish hopped on and began zipping around the room as if he were on a snowboard.

"Flying fish! Take cover!" the terrified Runt shrieked as he ducked under the bed.

"Fish!" Abby yelled, alarmed.

In a flash, Fish flew out the window into the night sky.

"No!" Chicken Little shouted as they all ran to the window. They watched as the twinkling panel flew straight up into the sky, leaving only Fish's trailing light stick visible as he vanished into the distance.

Abby, Runt, and Chicken Little raced down the stairs. They had no idea how or where they were going to find Fish, but they knew they had to get outside and look up at the sky. They needed to look for his light stick.

They were about to make a dash for the door when they found Buck standing at the bottom of the stairs.

"Wait, wait, whoa, whoa, whoa," Buck said to them. They screeched to a halt in front of him.

"Where's the fire here?" asked the big rooster.

Abby looked from Buck, who was still glowing from the day's big win, to a silent Chicken Little.

"Chicken Little has something to tell you!" she suddenly blurted out, overwhelmed by the urgency of Fish's fate.

Buck turned to his son. Chicken Little's head snapped toward Abby.

*"Tell him!"* Abby shouted. "He can handle it!"

Buck looked down at his son. Chicken Little stared up at his dad. How could he possibly explain about the star or the invisible panel or how Fish had just flown out the window? Would his father understand? Would he be happy? Would he—

"Who we talking about?" Chicken Little asked.

Buck shook his head in mild confusion as Chicken Little quickly led his friends out the front door.

Outside, the three friends broke into a full run. They could see Fish's green light stick moving across the dark sky.

"Sit tight, Fish!" Abby called as they darted through yards and hopped over fences.

"Fish! We will try to save you!" added Runt, who found bashing through the fences a lot easier than hopping over them. He was desperately huffing and puffing for air as he tried to keep up.

Together, they raced as fast as they could to catch up with the little green light stick until they found themselves in the middle of Oakey Oaks Stadium. The three stood on the pitcher's mound, completely out of breath. The light stick hung directly overhead.

Slowly, the light stick began to move in a wide arc. As it moved faster and faster, tracing a huge circle in the night sky, the stadium began to vibrate. The scoreboard numbers began to rattle. The bleacher seats began to wobble while the stadium lights flashed on and off.

Abby, Runt, and Chicken Little clung to one another as a sudden blinding light shined down on the pitcher's mound.

They looked up, trying to shield their eyes. A disklike craft was hovering above them.

Runt and Chicken Little ran for the dugout as the spinning ship lowered over the pitcher's mound. But Abby seemed unable to move. She stood in a daze on the field, her mouth open in disbelief and horror.

Chicken Little ran back to the pitcher's mound.

"Abby! Abby! Wake up!" he cried.

He grabbed her arm and pulled her toward the dugout.

"C'mon! Let's get out of here!" he shouted. A massive cloud of dust rose as the ship touched down. It was like a tornado!

The trio peeked out from the Acorns' dugout. Slowly, a hatch opened from the bottom of the ship. Runt, Abby, and Chicken Little held their breath as two huge terrifying spiderlike tentacled creatures emerged and headed toward the outfield.

As the creatures reached the edge of the outfield, the fence magically opened into a wide arch. The aliens proceeded through the arch and disappeared into the woods. Afterward, the arch collapsed and turned back into a fence.

"Poor Fish!" Runt wailed. He dropped his head into his hands. "He's gone. Gone, man!"

"Not yet," Abby said. She pointed to the top of the ship, where Fish was waving excitedly from a porthole.

"Oh, snap," Chicken Little said in shock. Things were definitely getting more complicated.

The brave trio overcame their fear and inched their way into the ship's open hatch. They had to save Fish!

The dark corridor they entered was lit only by glowing things and eerie electrical zaps that nearly caused Runt's heart to stop.

"Fish?" Chicken Little called out softly, but there was no answer.

Slowly, Abby, Runt, and Chicken Little crept past canisters holding strange and disturbing objects. Moving deeper into the dark ship, they passed vats of bubbling blue goo that seemed to have eyeballs floating in them. Something that looked like brains hovered nearby, floating in a strange energy beam.

Chicken Little noticed a small furry orange object suspended in a weird blue light shaft up ahead. He stopped for a moment and stared. Suddenly, in the middle of the orange fur . . . an eye opened! Chicken Little jumped back in surprise. He cocked his head, and the furry thing moved in the same direction inside its light shaft.

Was the creature copying him? He winked at it. The creature seemed to wink back. Fascinated, Chicken Little moved closer and—

"Hey!" Abby called. "What are you doing? Come on!"

Chicken Little turned and hurried after his friends.

Behind Chicken Little, the fuzzy creature was quiet for a moment. Then, suddenly, four tiny legs poked out from beneath the ball of fur. It hopped down and, hiding in the shadows, followed Chicken Little.

Chicken Little, Abby, and Runt continued cautiously down the hall. "Fish!" they whispered. "Fish!"

A bunch of dangling tentacles brushed over Runt's shoulder. It was more than the poor pig could take.

"Where are you, Fish?" he squealed frantically.

"*Shhh!* Quiet, Runt!" Chicken Little whispered loudly.

"I can't handle the pressure," Runt said, plastering himself against the wall. "Go on without me."

Abby put her hands on her hips. "Don't be silly; you're just fine!"

"I'll only jeopardize the mission!" Runt said dramatically. "Endanger us all! Throw me overboard while you still have the chance! Just leave me some ammo," he whimpered, "a little water...some chips if you have 'em."

"Calm, calm. Okay," said Abby. "All right."

"Runt," Chicken Little whispered, "where's your bag? Where's your bag?"

Runt reached down and fumbled around inside his sweater pocket until he pulled out a paper bag.

"Breathe," Chicken Little told him.

"Breathe," Abby instructed, and Runt put the bag up to his snout and breathed in and out to calm himself. Abby was reminding the pig of a tip she had learned about stress from one of her teen magazines.

Suddenly Runt inhaled the paper bag!

"Slowly! Slowly!" Chicken Little and Abby said.

Following his friends' advice, Runt finally calmed down enough to exhale the bag and move forward. The trio slowly continued down the dark corridor, searching for their lost friend.

"Fish," Chicken Little whispered hopefully. "Fish?"

Runt tried to be brave as sparks leaped and hot gasses hissed through the metal grates all around him. He began to sing softly to calm himself. Runt was feeling stronger, walking faster, feeling braver when he suddenly leaned back and screamed.

Abby and Chicken Little froze. Behind a wall-sized screen of slime was poor Fish's skeleton!

Runt pulled a second paper bag out of his pocket and took turns hyperventilating into each one.

"Fish!" Abby and Chicken Little cried.

The skeleton suddenly turned its head. Fish, in the flesh, stepped out from behind the X-ray screen of slime, waving cheerfully at his horrified pals.

"Are you okay?" Chicken Little asked as he and Abby rushed toward Fish. "Did they hurt you?"

"Say something!" Abby shouted as she tapped on Fish's face mask.

"Don't tap the glass," Chicken Little told her. "They hate it when you do that."

Abby flashed a look at Chicken Little. "All right. Let's get out of here," she said, glancing around. "Where's Runt?"

Fish blubbed and pointed. Both Abby and Chicken Little turned to see Runt, his mouth gaping in shock, standing in the light of a huge blinking map of the whole solar system. It looked like an attack plan of some sort. Planet after planet had been crossed out with a red *X*. Of all the planets, just one planet remained unmarked—but it had red arrows pointing to it from all sides. It was Earth. The aliens' plan was clear.

"We're next," Chicken Little said, gulping.

As soon as they recovered their wits, the four friends raced for the spaceship's exit hatch.

At that moment, the two large aliens were reentering the ship. They moved down the dark corridor but stopped short when they reached the blue light shaft where the orange fuzzy thing had winked at Chicken Little. The aliens' shrill cries filled the air. What was going on?

"That's it," whispered Abby when she heard the shrieks. "We're running back to your house and you are going to tell your dad."

"Okay, okay," Chicken Little finally agreed. "You're right, you're right."

Chicken Little and his friends, now completely terrified, sped down the hallway, turned a corner . . . and ran straight into the creepy aliens.

For a second, the aliens towered angrily over Chicken Little, Abby, Runt, and Fish. Then the four friends took off. They had to get to the hatch and escape! The aliens took up the chase.

As the friends reached the exit hatch, Chicken Little pushed a red button on the wall, closing a door between them and the angry aliens. Fish dove out the hatch first. Runt tried to follow but got stuck in the hatch doorway.

"It wasn't this tight coming in," the pig grunted.

"We gotta get out of here, right now!" shouted Chicken Little, pressing the red button repeatedly. "Come on, you guys!" The aliens were very close. Chicken Little had his finger on the button, struggling to hold the door closed while the aliens struggled to open it.

Abby tried her best to push Runt through as Fish pulled the poor pig's dangling feet. Finally, with a giant thud, Runt plopped to the ground. Abby and Chicken Little tumbled out behind him. Without Chicken Little pushing the button, the aliens were finally able to get through the door, and they followed the friends down through the open hatch.

"Come on, guys! Hurry, hurry, hurry!" Chicken Little urged his friends toward the woods outside the ball field. But Fish had other ideas. The happy-go-lucky little guy was still under the hatch, jumping up, playfully trying to grab the aliens' tentacles. Fish liked everybody—even dangerous, attacking aliens.

Chicken Little and Abby watched in shock as Runt bravely ran back, grabbed Fish by the helmet, and took off with him under his arm. They were impressed. No paper bag for Runt this time!

The aliens dropped from the ship's hatch and began to chase Abby, Runt, Fish, and Chicken Little deep into the forest of Oakey Oaks.

Back at the spaceship, all was quiet for a moment. Then the tiny fuzzy orange creature appeared at the exit hatch. It, too, jumped down to the ground and quickly followed the group.

Far into the forest, Chicken Little turned to see the aliens using their long tentacles to swing from tree to tree, like gigantic monkeys. The creepy red-eyed aliens chased the friends to the very top of a hill.

Abby, Fish, Runt, and Chicken Little took one step over the dark rise and tumbled, head over heels, all the way down into a cornfield. They scrambled to their feet and ran down the long rows of corn to hide.

The aliens stopped at the edge of the field. They turned on two huge searchlights and scanned the cornfield, but there was no sign of Chicken Little and his friends.

Hiding under a cornstalk, Chicken Little let out a small sigh of relief. Maybe the aliens would just give up and never come back. Maybe no one would ever have to know that this had happened. Then he saw the two aliens floating toward them. *Maybe it's time for a new plan,* he thought as each of the aliens' tentacles turned into a sharp spinning blade, instantly mowing the corn down to the ground like a living lawn mower.

The four terrified friends leaped to their feet and ran, darting through rows of corn, trying to stay out of sight. They zigzagged through the cornfield, dodging the alien searchlights.

"The school bell!" Abby yelled, spotting the bell tower beyond the cornfield. "We've got to ring the school bell to warn everyone! Come on!"

At last, the little gang reached the school. Desperately, they yanked on the doors. "It's locked," Abby cried as Runt began to make whimpering sounds. The aliens' bright searchlights were getting closer!

Chicken Little looked up at the bell tower. "I need a soda," he declared in a moment of inspiration.

"Come on, buddy! Come on, buddy!" Chicken Little chanted

as he tried to put a crumpled dollar bill into his old faithful soda machine. The dollar bill buzzed into the machine, then buzzed right back out.

"The corner's all wrinkled," Runt said, staring at the dollar.

"Why are we doing this?" Abby asked.

Runt was as confused as Abby, but he was still determined to get the bill into the machine. "Take it! Take it!" he begged the machine. In complete desperation, Runt slammed the machine with his full weight, then lifted it up in fury. Dented and scarred, the machine finally gave up, and a soda bottle rolled out. It was exactly what Chicken Little needed.

Chicken Little shook the bottle, threw it over his shoulder, and kicked off the cap. Just like the last time, the bottle propelled him straight up into the air. Abby, Runt, and Fish were amazed.

As he flew upward, Chicken Little reached out for the bell rope but couldn't quite make it. Instead, he grabbed the ledge just below the bell . . . then fell back down to a windowsill even farther below, where the soda bottle had landed.

Chicken Little looked up. He had accidentally loosened a brick in the tower, and it was about to fall right on top of him! He quickly moved aside and pushed the bottle underneath him as Abby and Runt held their breath. The brick fell and hit the plastic bottle, whooshing the air out of it and launching Chicken Little straight up.

This time, he caught the rope. Then he stopped.

Chicken Little knew he had to ring the bell *now,* but he couldn't help remembering the last time he'd been here. His mind flashed back to the day he'd been hit on the head by something, then had run to this very tower and yelled, "The sky is falling! The sky is falling!"

He remembered his neighbors running in panic, the mass destruction he had caused, and the mayor yelling, "It's only an acorn!" as everyone laughed at him. He also remembered how ashamed his dad had been.

Suddenly, a scream snapped him back to the present. His friends were trapped in the aliens' spotlights.

"AHHHHHHH!" Abby yelled in terror.

Chicken Little pulled the bell rope with all his might. DONG! DONG! DONG! DONG!

As the sound of the bell reverberated, the aliens trembled

and grabbed their heads with their tentacles. Something about the noise bothered them. Though they were hesitant, they retreated, unseen, scurrying back into the cornfield.

Meanwhile, not far away, the fuzzy little orange creature covered its tiny ears, too. Then it burrowed into the ground for extra safety.

DONG! DONG! The bell rang out all over Oakey Oaks. Buck Cluck, dozing in his recliner in front of the TV, heard it. Even the weatherman on Buck's TV heard it. Citizens in their coops, barns, and stalls stopped what they were doing. *The bell?* they wondered. The townsfolk began to gather in the streets and race toward the school. There must be a true emergency!

Mayor Turkey Lurkey led the frantic crowd to the school. Then he looked up and saw Chicken Little on the bell tower.

"Chicken Little, you'd better have a good explanation for this!" one of the townsfolk yelled, not happy with the situation.

"There's . . . there's, it's a—you have to—d'oh!" Chicken Little stammered, trying to explain. The crowd was totally confused. That was when Chicken Little realized that this was too big and difficult to explain. He climbed down from the bell tower and faced the gathering. “Follow me!” he shouted, taking command.

But the crowd didn’t move. They looked to the mayor to see what they should do next. “C’mon!” Chicken Little said to the mayor boldly. “Hurry! Hurry!”

“There’s a chain of command here,” the mayor gobbled. “Mayors first!” The crowd surged forward to follow Chicken Little and the mayor.

But just as Chicken Little reached the gates to enter the ball field, the mayor stopped abruptly and leaned over. The whole crowd stopped behind him.

“Ooh, look!” the mayor said excitedly. “A penny!”

Chicken Little looked over his shoulder at the crowd.

“Guys!” he called out desperately.

“Oh, right,” the mayor called back as he quickly put the shiny new penny in his pocket and moved onward.

“Hurry!” Chicken Little yelled to the townsfolk. He was the only one inside the stadium. The spaceship was clearly visible. One of the aliens was even peeking out of the ship’s dome. Chicken Little needed the townsfolk there now, or they would miss seeing the spaceship altogether!

But the crowd was still outside. And by the time the townsfolk got to the gates of the baseball field, Chicken Little was frantic.

"Come on, quick! It's taking off!" Chicken Little pleaded. Behind him, he could hear the hum of the spaceship warming up its engines.

# Chapter 20

As the townsfolk finally poured through the big gates, they found . . . nothing. It was too late. The aliens and their ship had disappeared.

Chicken Little couldn't believe they were gone. "Okay, I know this looks bad," he said to the crowd nervously, "but there's an invisible spaceship right there. With aliens who are here to invade Earth."

The crowd stared at Chicken Little in disbelief. To prove his story, he picked up a small rock and threw it at where the spaceship had been just moments before. The rock fell to the ground with barely a sound. It definitely had not hit a spaceship.

"Okay," Chicken Little said. "We all know I don't have a very good arm. But you see, there are these cloaking panels on the bottom that make it disappear. And I know this because one fell out of the sky and hit me on the head."

A cheetah groaned. "Oh, it's the acorn thing all over again."

The news crew packed up their equipment. "There's no story here," the cameraman said in disgust.

Chicken Little desperately looked into the angry faces of his neighbors. "I'm telling you, everybody! It was here!"

Buck put his hand over his face as the crowd began to grumble.

"No, wait!" Abby pleaded. "There *were* aliens!"

"Yeah," Runt said, doing his best alien imitation. "They had three big red eyes, and claws and hooks and tentacles, and they were big—"

Suddenly, Runt's gigantic mother approached. "Runt! That's enough!" she squealed in a warning tone. Without asking her son for an explanation, she grabbed the young pig by the ear and dragged him away.

Chicken Little knew he had to convince the townsfolk. "Everybody! I'm telling the truth!" he insisted. In desperation, he appealed to Buck. "Dad," he said, looking up at his father. "I'm not making this up! You gotta believe me this time."

Buck was silent for a moment. Every eye in the crowd was glaring at him. He cleared his throat.

"No, son," he sighed. "I don't."

The big rooster turned to the crowd.

"I can't tell you how embarrassed I am, folks," he said. "I'm really sorry about this, everyone. It looks like this is just a big, crazy misunderstanding."

"Well, other than the penny," the mayor declared as he reached into his pocket and showed everyone the shiny coin, "this whole evening was a flop!"

The townsfolk grumbled and turned to go home. They had had enough of Chicken Little and all the trouble he caused with his false alarms.

"Oh, Mr. Cluck," a sickeningly sweet voice said. It was none other than Foxy Loxy, devious as usual. "Don't take it so hard. No one blames you."

Chicken Little watched sadly as Buck walked off with Foxy. Abby tried to offer her friend a sympathetic look, but she realized he simply needed to be alone for a while. As she turned in one direction, he turned the other way and walked into the darkness by himself.

Meanwhile, in the cornfield, the little fuzzy orange creature crawled out of the hole it had dug in the dirt and sadly watched a streak of light—the spaceship—disappear into the sky, leaving it behind.

A few minutes later, the frightened little fuzzball followed the single creature it recognized. It was Chicken Little. And even though Chicken Little never saw the little creature, the fuzzball followed him all the way home to the Cluck house.

The next morning at the Cluck home, Buck was frantically answering phone calls while the television news blared in the background, retelling all the events of the previous night . . . as well as detailing the destruction and harm that had occurred as a result.

"Reports of panic and mayhem are still pouring in after yet another Chicken Little incident last night," the reporter was saying. "In one instance, an entire family of lemmings was sent running in fear, but unable to find a cliff, they instead began throwing themselves from the nearest park bench."

Buck held the phone to his ear as his cell phone also began to ring. He answered one call after another.

"Hello. . . . I'm sorry."

"Hello. . . . I apologize."

"Hello? Please forgive me."

Buck apologized to one caller after another. His computer suddenly flashed and said cheerfully, "You have hate mail!"

"What are you saying, sir?" Buck said, now juggling both phones. He stuck his head out the window. "Oh, yes, I do see the skywriting there!"

Buck began to read the message in the sky. He was stunned by how unkind the message was—or, at least, how unkind it was meant to be. "Thank goodness the cloud blocked the last letter!" he muttered.

As Buck struggled to manage the chaos inside the Cluck home, Chicken Little sat alone in the backyard, trying to figure out where it all had gone wrong.

Suddenly, a magazine dropped next to him. On the cover was the word "Talk." Chicken Little looked up into the faces of Abby, Runt, and Fish. His best friends looked worried.

"If ever there was a time to talk to your dad, it's now," Abby announced, picking up the magazine.

Chicken Little shook his head. "It's too late for that."

Runt began to whimper and sing a song he thought fit everyone's mood.

"Runt!" Abby said. Runt stopped singing and resorted to a sad, soft crying sound.

Chicken Little sighed. Then he thought he heard Runt whimpering again. "Runt, I just really want to be alone right now," he told his friend.

As his friends walked away, Chicken Little realized what he had been hearing. It wasn't Runt at all. The little fuzzy orange thing from the spaceship was right next to him, and it seemed to be crying. The whimpering sounds quickly turned to wailing, and before Chicken Little knew it, the ball of fuzz was throwing a full-blown fit. It was babbling and gurgling hysterically. Chicken Little shrieked, jumping back in terror.

Hearing the commotion, Abby, Runt, and Fish rushed back into the yard.

"What is that thing?" Runt howled, seeing the alien creature. Abby joined in the screaming as Fish moved closer and offered the creature a gentle "Blub."

The little alien seemed to respond. Fish held up a fin to silence his screaming friends. As soon as they calmed down, the fuzzball began to babble.

"Blub," Fish answered understandingly.

The creature continued to babble even more loudly.

Chicken Little, Abby, and Runt began to understand. The little orange blob wasn't an "it" but a "he." He was a tiny creature with feelings, just like them!

"Blub-blub," Fish said, encouraging him to continue.

The orange ball became very excited and motioned toward the sky with a big *shwoooo* sound.

*"Blub!"* Fish gasped. He understood everything the little guy was saying.

Fish turned to his friends. "Blub," he said matter-of-factly.

"It came from the spaceship?" Chicken Little asked.

"They left him behind?" Abby was wondering, too.

Finally, Chicken Little said to the little alien, "Don't cry. We're here for you. We're going to do whatever it takes to get you back home, okay?"

The poor little alien was harmless and frightened from being left behind by his parents. Chicken Little was just beginning to think about what to do next when the sky began to rumble.

# Chapter 22

Buck ran from the house and looked up. The sky appeared to be cracking apart. In fact, it was a fleet of cloaked spaceships that were separating high above the town, making the sky seem as if it were breaking up. One after another, spaceships began to descend over Oakey Oaks. Townsfolk ran into the streets, panicked. It was a full-on alien invasion!

Meanwhile, the fuzzy alien happily looked up at the ships and babbled at Fish as fast as he could.

"Blub!" Fish answered with a smile.

"Those are your parents?" Chicken Little asked the happy little alien.

The creature gurgled enthusiastically.

"And they brought the galactic armada?" Chicken Little asked, looking up at the ominous spacecrafts.

The little alien kid scurried down the street as the spaceships began to near the ground. Cars swerved in all directions to avoid hitting him.

“Watch out for the kid! Don’t hit him!” Chicken Little yelled as one car almost got the orange ball of fur.

Chicken Little was about to chase the furry alien when Buck suddenly grabbed his arm. He had been looking for his son. “You were right,” Buck said quickly as he prepared to save Chicken Little. “Alien invasion. I see that now.”

Chicken Little took a deep breath. “Yeah, you know, about that . . . It’s actually just a rescue mission!” He tried to explain quickly. “This alien kid was left behind by mistake, and they’re just coming back to get him. So we have to help him, Dad, because if we don’t, who else will?”

“What!” Buck exclaimed.

Chicken Little stopped. He recognized that look on his dad’s face. “Forget it,” he said, taking off down the street after the young alien. “You wouldn’t believe me anyway.”

Buck began to chase after him. “Come back! Son!”

Abby, Runt, and Fish ran down the street, too. “Mr. Cluck, wait!” Abby yelled. “He’s telling the truth!”

“He is!” Runt added. “Though given his track record, we understand why you don’t believe him!”

Meanwhile, in one of the ships, the orange alien's parents were nervously awaiting news of their lost child. "Is there any sign of him?" they asked their pilot.

"Negative," the pilot answered. "We'll have to send in the ground troops."

Far below, on the ground, the citizens of Oakey Oaks watched in horror as countless metallic aliens dropped from the ships. Foxy Loxy and Gooscy Loosey were in the town square.

"Run away! Run away!" one of the townsfolk yelled as the crowd dispersed.

Suddenly, a huge alien landed face to face with Foxy. As much a bully as ever, Foxy stepped back, picked up a rock, and prepared to throw. Following Foxy's lead, as usual, Goosey leaned forward and picked up a rock of her own, ready to launch it with full force.

Foxy threw her rock as hard as she could, but it bounced harmlessly off the alien. It was probably the biggest mistake of Foxy's life. In response, the alien zapped her with a light beam. Goosey Loosey's jaw dropped as Foxy disappeared into thin air. Goosey gently put her rock back on the ground and ran off into the crowd as the alien watched her.

Meanwhile, the fuzzy alien kid was zigzagging through the mayhem, trying to get to his parents' ship. A huge truck barreled toward the little creature. Chicken Little saw that the little orange alien was about to be hit.

Quickly, Chicken Little jumped onto a car, bent the antenna back like a catapult, and launched himself through the air. Zooming straight ahead, he grabbed the furry alien kid as he whizzed by, and they flew right through the doors of the Oakey Oaks movie theater. They shot over the seats and—*smack*—right into the movie screen.

Sliding down the screen, Chicken Little heard his dad's voice. Worried about his son, Buck had raced after him. The little fuzzball was frightened by the big rooster and hid behind the theater curtains.

"Where's your head?" Buck yelled, wondering if Chicken Little had lost his mind. He didn't realize that Chicken Little was trying to rescue an innocent alien child. "We gotta get outta here!"

The sounds of the alien invasion outside rocked the theater.

Suddenly, Abby burst through the theater doors. She saw Chicken Little and his dad onstage having an argument.

"You with the running, and the jumping—" Buck complained, trying to drag his son to safety.

"Dad, no! Wait!"

"What are you guys doing?" Abby shouted. "We gotta get out of here!" She didn't understand them at all. Why were they wasting time arguing when the whole town was falling apart under an alien invasion?

She stomped her webbed foot. "Will you two stop messing around and deal with the problem?" She finally got their attention.

Chicken Little looked at his dad for a moment. "You're never there for me!" he blurted out.

Abby was stunned. What a time for Chicken Little to take the advice from her teen magazines!

"Wha—?" Buck said.

"You're never there for me," Chicken Little said, mustering up his courage. "I mean, you were there when I won the big game but not when I thought the sky fell and not at the ball field, and certainly not now."

"Okay," Abby said, "that's not what I had in mind, but this is good! Keep going, keep going!"

"You've been ashamed of me ever since the acorn thing happened. And we have to talk about it," Chicken Little continued. He was on a roll now.

Buck looked into Chicken Little's eyes. What could he say? "I—I didn't realize, son." He sighed. "Son, I never meant to—the acorn, the sky... You're right. Your mom, she was always good with stuff like this. Me, I'm going to need a lot of work. You need to know that I love you, no matter what. And I'm sorry if I ever made you feel like that was something you had to earn."

The two hugged as Abby announced, "*And* . . . we're good! Let's go. Let's go!"

"Okay, Dad," Chicken Little said as he pulled back the curtain, "all we gotta do is return this helpless little kid."

The scared little alien struck a karate pose and jumped atop Buck's head, biting him with impressive gusto.

"This orange bitey thing needs saving?" Buck asked as he tried to shake the alien loose. "I never heard of such a crazy,

crazy . . ." Buck saw his son's face drop, so he quickly changed his tone. "Crazy, *wonderful* idea! Just tell me what you need me to do!"

Chicken Little brightened like a lightbulb.

"You really mean it?" he asked Buck.

"You bet!" Buck answered, holding the orange bitey thing at arm's length. The alien continued to gnaw his fingers. "Anything, son."

Chicken Little hopped off the stage and marched toward the door. "C'mon, Dad. We've got a planet to save!"

Buck muttered as the little alien kept snapping at him. "Crazy supportive—that's me!"

The alien managed to grab a few feathers in his teeth and pulled hard.

"OW!" Buck yelled. "This thing likes to nibble, doesn't it?"

Chicken Little suddenly turned and ran back down the aisle toward Abby. He hopped onto a chair and looked Abby right in the eye.

"By the way," he told her, "I would like to say I've always found you extremely attractive!"

Then he took the stunned duck in his arms and planted a big kiss on her beak.

None of her teen magazines had prepared her for this. Abby smiled dreamily. "Now *that's* closure!"

But on the streets of Oakey Oaks, Buck, Abby, and Chicken Little found a full-blown alien invasion under way.

Running through the mayhem, Runt and Fish spotted their friends exiting the theater. "Wait!" Runt called to Abby. "What's going on?"

Runt saw the love-struck daze in Abby's eyes. "Ah!" he squealed to Fish. "They've given her an alien mind wipe!"

Lasers flashed throughout the town square as a huge mechanical alien walker passed by city hall. With five long spiderlike legs and three angry red eyes, it looked similar to the aliens that had chased Chicken Little through the cornfield earlier—but this one was shooting laser beams at everyone. Mayor Turkey Lurkey was frantic.

Buck turned to Chicken Little. "Okay, son. What do we do now?" he asked.

"It's a piece of cake, Dad. All we have to do is take the kid down the street to the giant metal alien!" Chicken Little said as he took off across the town square with the orange creature in his arms.

"We surrender!" the mayor yelled up to the alien. "Here, here. Take the key to the city!"

The alien walker blasted the key from the mayor's hands. But the alien didn't seem to be finished with the mayor, and that made the turkey nervous.

"Key to my car?" the mayor asked, fumbling in his pockets. He even offered the alien a breath mint.

Finally, the mayor had nothing left to offer. In an instant, he disappeared in a zap of laser fire.

"Forget plan A!" Chicken Little yelled as he turned around and ran back to Buck.

From above, the alien walker spotted the young orange alien. The little furball began to babble as the big alien scoped out the situation. Using his internal positioning radar, he zeroed in on Buck's face as the big rooster spoke to the babbling alien child. A blast of alien fire suddenly shot down between Buck and Chicken Little. The chicken family had been targeted by the attacking aliens! They jumped out of the way and raced down the street as alien sirens began screaming from the huge spiderlike walker.

Chicken Little and Buck ducked into a parked car.

"Okay, what now, son, who, by the way, I support one hundred percent?"

Out of breath, Chicken Little handed the fuzzy alien back to his dad and said, "Plan B!"

"Of course," Buck agreed. "Plan B!" Then he turned to his son. "What is plan B?"

The little alien started gesturing frantically. Buck asked, "You have to go to the bathroom? You want juice? A snack? Corn dog?" He sighed hopelessly. "Oh, I stink at this. I'm a horrible father."

The kid shook his little head in frustration and climbed onto Buck's shoulders. He twisted Buck's head to see a spaceship hovering over the town hall. Buck finally began to get the idea. So did Chicken Little.

"Oh, is that your parents?" Chicken Little said in surprise.

The creature nodded excitedly and happily gurgled with all his might.

“That’s it, Dad!” Chicken Little exclaimed. “Plan B! All we have to do is duck and weave through traffic, and make our way through town square while avoiding the death rays from those alien robots; then we get to town hall, climb up to the highest point on the roof, and give the kid back to his parents.”

“Yeah!” Buck agreed as he threw open the car door. But his expression was far from enthusiastic.

"Charge!" Buck yelled as he and Chicken Little took off. With Chicken Little leading the way and Buck carrying the little alien, they raced through the mayhem. Suddenly, Buck tripped and the furry creature went flying. But Chicken Little didn't miss a beat. He caught the alien kid in his little arms and kept running.

The alien walkers quickly fixed Chicken Little and the fuzzy alien in their sights and began vaporizing cars in front and in back of them.

Buck and Chicken Little finally reached town hall but realized they were surrounded by aliens.

"Okay, son, now what?" Buck asked.

"Fire truck!" Chicken Little yelled, pointing directly at an oncoming vehicle. The fire truck zoomed into the town square. Runt was at the wheel, although he didn't quite fit in the driver's seat; his rear end hung out the window.

With help from Abby, Runt steered the fire truck over to Buck and Chicken Little and picked them up just as an alien blast vaporized the spot where they'd been standing.

"Plan C!" yelled Chicken Little and Buck together.

Fish hung out the window and rang the bell as the truck zoomed out of the town square.

"Runt, turn around," Chicken Little yelled. "Go back to town hall!"

"But they'll *vaporize* us!" Runt screamed.

"Runt, just do it!" Chicken Little shouted. "It will work. We will survive."

Runt gritted his teeth and yelled, "Brake, Abby! Floor it!"

The back end of the truck swung around as the tires screeched. Suddenly, the fire truck was facing the alien invaders. Abby hit the gas. The truck barreled forward as the aliens started firing wildly at them.

Buck screamed as every blast missed the truck by inches.

The alien walkers moved steadily toward the truck. They were closing in like huge spiders on a helpless fly.

Fish quickly climbed out the window and released the truck's ladder. It swung out in a wide arc, hitting the aliens' spiderlike legs. One by one, the aliens toppled to the street.

*"Rrrrarrr!"* Fish yelled, waving his fins.

*"Woo hoo!"* Runt cheered, but then he looked up and saw that they were about to hit town hall. He screamed as the truck crashed into the steps. Buck, Chicken Little, and the alien kid were thrown from the truck into the town hall. It was an odd way to enter the building, but it worked. Landing next to the building's broken elevator, Buck pointed to the stairs. "Plan D!"

It was thirty flights of stairs to the top of town hall. By the fifteenth floor, Buck couldn't take another step.

"Thighs burning . . . feet hurting." Buck gasped for breath. And he also remembered his new decision to treat his son with respect and dignity. "But loving you! Full support!" he groaned with as much enthusiasm as he could muster.

Chicken Little and the fuzzy alien kid pulled the wheezing rooster along until they finally reached the top of the building. Chicken Little spotted a small door that led to its large gold dome. He and the alien kid popped through the door and onto the dome. But Buck got stuck going through.

"I can't get out," the rooster said as he desperately tried to push himself through. "Come back, son! We can't go out this way. It's too dangerous!" he called to Chicken Little.

"No, Dad, I can do this! I can do this," protested Chicken Little. "You've got to believe me this time."

Buck thought for a moment. But it was just a moment. He realized that it was time to trust his boy.

"Go to it, son!" he said.

Chicken Little scaled the side of the dome, holding the alien child tightly. Under the ship's blinding white lights, Chicken Little stood alone, lifting the little orange alien high over his head.

"Here's your kid!" he yelled up to the ship. "Look! Over here!"

Buck saw two squads of aliens coming at Chicken Little, climbing up from both sides of the tower. His son was in danger! And that was all Buck needed to know. Using all his strength, the big rooster burst through the little door onto the roof. "Son—son! I'm here, son!" Buck yelled.

An alien with its weapon drawn was rushing toward Chicken Little and the tiny orange creature.

"Get away from my boy!" Buck roared.

The big rooster was on a serious mission now. In a matter of seconds, he, Chicken Little, and the alien child were completely surrounded.

Then, from the ship, a laser beam vaporized all three of them into thin air.

In a blinding flash, Chicken Little, Buck, and the little alien instantly rematerialized in an eerie chamber deep inside the ship. They were helpless, floating weightlessly in the chamber, along with all the others who had been zapped. Buck was clutching the orange alien kid.

*Uh-oh,* Buck thought as a giant viewing screen snapped on, displaying three huge alien eyes. The furry red creature on the screen glared at them angrily.

"WHY DID YOU TAKE OUR CHILD?" it asked in a deep, booming voice.

"Hey, just hold on there, buddy," Buck replied. "My son did not take your kid. You were the one who left him behind, and that's bad parenting. And I should know."

"SILENCE!" the big scary voice commanded. "RELEASE THE CHILD!"

Buck gently let go of the alien child. The little furry guy hovered in midair and then slowly sank to the floor.

Buck and Chicken Little watched as the ball extended all of his thin little legs. He quickly waddled to the side of the chamber and through a small door, which instantly closed behind him. Buck and Chicken Little sighed. They were relieved that the alien was back with his parents at last. But their relief didn't last long.

"YOU HAVE VIOLATED INTERGALACTIC LAW 90210," the voice announced. "A CHARGE PUNISHABLE BY IMMEDIATE PARTICLE DISINTEGRATION!"

Big alien guns were drawn, surrounding Buck and Chicken Little. Then another screen popped up. This one had the alien child's eyes on it.

"Ba da da bee do boo," the orange creature gurgled.

"HMM? WHAT'S THAT?" the loud voice said to the young alien. The little alien kept gurgling.

"HMM," the deep voice said, sounding confused. "I DON'T QUITE . . ."

A third viewing screen snapped on. Three female eyes set in yellow fur began to blink slowly.

"Melvin, honey," a woman's voice said calmly from the new screen, "he's saying they're telling the truth."

“UH . . . HUH,” the deep voice mumbled.

“It was just a misunderstanding,” the soft female voice continued.

“Bub-bo,” the little orange alien added.

“WELL, THEN,” the red alien said. “THIS IS AWKWARD, HUH?”

“Yes, it is,” his alien wife, Tina, answered, fluttering her eyelashes.

“I SUPPOSE I SHOULD . . .”

“Put the big guns away?” Tina finished for her husband.

“OH, OF COURSE,” he said, immediately following his wife’s instructions.

“And turn off your Big Voice,” she said next.

“BUT I DON’T—”

“Turn it off,” Tina insisted.

“BUT I DON’T GET TO USE THE BIG VOICE VERY OFTEN,” Melvin said. Then, hesitating, he finally gave in. “YES, DEAR,” he sighed.

Moments later, the alien family stood outside the ship in Oakey Oaks along with Buck and Chicken Little. Melvin seemed pleased as he looked around the town square. His alien associates were busy using their lasers to restore the rubble back to its prevaporized state. Every inch of Oakey Oaks was almost as good as new.

And now that Melvin and Tina weren't wearing their big metal walking suits with tentacles and sharp blades, the two aliens did not seem scary at all. In fact, they were almost cute. They were furry and colorful and looked a lot like their orange child, only a bit bigger.

"Again, I cannot tell you how sorry we are for this whole misunderstanding," Melvin told Buck cheerfully.

Tina smiled and spoke with sincerity. "Oh, goodness, we are so very sorry!"

Melvin shook his head and laughed. "If it hadn't been for your son there, we might have vaporized the whole planet!"

"What?" Buck said in shock. Around them, all the townsfolk gasped. They realized not only that their whole planet had almost been destroyed but also that Chicken Little—yes, Chicken Little!—had saved the day. Chicken Little was in shock. Had he actually done something right? And the rest of the townsfolk were looking at him with newfound admiration. This was more than a lucky hit on the baseball field—the tiny troublemaking chicken had saved them all.

"And, oh, my goodness, what a shame that would have been," Tina said, going back to how they had almost destroyed Earth. "I mean, where else would we have picked our acorns?"

Melvin nodded. "We stop here every summer," he said, "on the way to the in-laws'."

He pulled out a map of the galaxy. Several planets had been crossed out, and Earth had a big red circle around it.

"We looked on all the other planets," Melvin explained. "You can only find them here on Earth."

Chicken Little remembered the map. It was the same one he and his friends had seen inside the spaceship. It suddenly dawned on the little chicken that Earth was just one more stop on an intergalactic shopping trip. It had not been targeted by the aliens to be destroyed. He let out a small sigh.

Chicken Little and Buck exchanged looks. Chicken Little couldn't help wondering if the aliens' annual acorn trip had something to do with the acorn that had hit him on the head the year before.

The whine of an alien rescue siren interrupted the conversation. An alien pulled up and opened the hatch of his vehicle. He quickly stepped out and faced Melvin.

"Okay," he said, reporting to Melvin, "everything's been put back to normal . . . except for this one over here." The commander pointed over his shoulder.

Everyone turned. It was Foxy...or at least someone who looked kind of like Foxy.

Chicken Little's jaw dropped. In shock, he adjusted his large green-rimmed glasses as he looked at a charming little fox with curls wearing a pink dress. She had bows in her hair, rosy pink cheeks, and a coat of lipstick so thick you could have lost your homework in it.

Foxy giggled and smiled coquettishly.

"Hi, y'all," she said.

Chicken Little, Abby, and Runt were speechless. It was a makeover that even the beauty experts at the Fox Salon could never have managed.

One of the aliens tried to explain apologetically. "She got her brain waves a little scrambled during reconstitution." He almost seemed as shocked by her appearance as her fellow townsfolk were.

Foxy batted her long eyelashes as she sang a little tune. Runt felt his heart skip a few beats.

"But no worries," the rescue commander continued. He was talking mostly to Melvin. "We can put her back the way she was."

Melvin was just about to reply when he heard a voice behind him.

"No!" Runt said quickly, and sighed. "She's perfect."

Foxy did a little twirl, singing to no one in particular. Runt was enchanted and began to sing along with her.

The rescue commander stared at the strange pink fox twirling next to the giant love-struck pig.

"Scary," the alien said, shrugging.

Melvin's wristwatch beeped.

"Whoops, darling!" he said, glancing down at it. "Look at the time! We better get a move on!"

Tina nodded while Melvin smiled, reached out, and shook Chicken Little's hand.

"All right, then," he said. "It was good meeting you. Sorry for the whole full-scale invasion thing, but hey, I'm a dad. You know how it is with your kids; when they need you, you do whatever it takes."

Buck smiled and had to agree. *Guess it's the same for families everywhere,* he thought. He put an arm around Chicken Little as the aliens walked up the ramp to the ship.

Suddenly, a panel from underneath the ship came loose and clanged to the ground.

Melvin's wife shot him a look.

"There goes that panel again," she said. "Every year we come here, this thing falls off. Seriously, honey, someday it is going to hit somebody on the head."

She picked up the panel and pressed a button on the back.

It rose into the air and hovered for a moment, then snapped back into place on the underside of the ship.

Chicken Little and Buck stopped thinking about the acorn and focused on the panel. Obviously, the panels were the "pieces of sky" that had fallen on Chicken Little. Twice.

"NONSENSE!" Melvin boomed to Tina. "THE CHANCES OF THAT HAPPENING ARE ONE MILLION TO ONE!"

"Melvin, did you just try to use the Big Voice on me?" Tina asked as they rose into the humming spacecraft.

"I, UH . . . WHO WE TALKING ABOUT?" Melvin asked as the hatch of the ship began to close.

The little alien kid rose into the spaceship, too.

"Bye-bye!" he said, waving to Chicken Little.

Buck and Chicken Little watched as the ship flashed a blinding blue light, then disappeared into the sky.

Within the year, Chicken Little and his three friends found themselves sitting inside the dark movie theater, along with all the townsfolk of Oakey Oaks. They were watching an amazing adventure saga entitled *Chicken Little: The True Story*.

A booming voice on the huge screen yelled, "Red alert! Man your battle stations. Status report, Mr. Fish!"

"Commander Little," the fish answered clearly, "the evil FoxLoxian army has broken through the planet's atmosphere."

A lovely duck on-screen looked alarmed. "But that means—"

"Yes, I know," the big muscular chicken on the screen said gravely. "The sky"—he took a pause for effect—"is falling."

"Commander Little," the duck cried, "no!"

"Please. Call me Ace," the heroic screen chicken replied.

"Oh, Ace! No!"

The chicken swept the duck into his big arms. "I never intended to bring you into this, Abby."

He turned to the transmission screen and spoke to the bravest member of his crew. “Runt, do you copy?”

“Yes, Commander?” the dashing young pig answered from his fighter craft.

“Runt, my friend, an alien fleet is about to invade Earth. Civilization as we know it depends on me and, to a lesser extent, you. So I’ve got just one question for you.” The chicken paused for a moment, then asked, “Are you ready to rock?”

Runt smiled and shifted the bill of his tiny cap to the back. The fearless pig began singing a jaunty tune as his spaceship zoomed forward.

The chicken smiled. He knew that if he could count on anyone to put his bacon on the line, it was Runt. “Raise your pork shield, Runt. Prepare to engage!”

Runt and the valiant chicken flew their spaceships side by side, blasting their lasers. They were up against all of the FoxLoxian armada.

“Stay on target! Stay on target!” the chicken shouted.

A huge explosion sent shock waves through both ships.

“Runt! Runt, are you all right?” the heroic chicken yelled

desperately, fearing for his friend's life.

"No, no," the brave pig gasped into his headset. "Ya gotta go on without me, Commander. Just leave me some ammo, a little water . . . some chips if you have 'em."

"This is amazingly accurate!" a thrilled Runt whispered enthusiastically from his theater seat.

"Bloop!" Fish said, nodding, as the two smiled and ate their popcorn.

"He was my good friend," the Chicken Little character continued on-screen, watching the pig's flaming fighter drift into space. "Oh, Abby, at least I still have you. Abby . . ."

Sitting next to each other in the dark theater, Chicken Little and Abby reached for popcorn at the same moment. Their hands touched—and both pulled back, embarrassed. But then, as they turned their faces back to the screen, they happily slipped their hands together.

Up on the big movie screen, the lovely duck sighed, "Ace . . ."

"Abby . . . ," the handsome chicken answered, gazing into her soft duck eyes.

The duck draped her arms around the chicken's neck as they stood in front of the smoking ruins of town hall. The Oakey Oaks flag was waving behind them.

"Good people of Oakey Oaks," the brave chicken said with his head held high, "though at times it may feel like the sky is falling around you, never give up. For every day is a new day!"

The gallant chicken thumbed the controls of his jet-pak and lifted into the sky, revealing his origami pants. The words "The End" flashed across the screen.

The crowd in the theater jumped to their feet and cheered loudly. The folks of Oakey Oaks had finally found themselves a real hero.

The movie was all Buck and Chicken Little could have hoped for—maybe even a little more. But the best part wasn't up on the screen. It was in their hearts. It was in the simple truth that Chicken Little finally knew his father was proud of him and loved him. No matter what.